TROUBLE AT
FORT LA POINTE

by
Kathleen Ernst

American Girl™

Published by Pleasant Company Publications
Text Copyright © 2000 by Kathleen Ernst
Illustrations Copyright © 2000 by Pleasant Company
For information, address: Book Editor, Pleasant Company Publications,
8400 Fairway Place, P.O. Box 620998, Middleton, WI 53562.

Printed in the United States of America.
00 01 02 03 04 05 RRD 10 9 8 7 6 5 4 3 2 1

History Mysteries® and American Girl®
are trademarks of Pleasant Company.

PERMISSIONS & PICTURE CREDITS
The following individuals and organizations have generously given permission to reprint
illustrations contained in "A Peek into the Past": p. 155—*Ojibwe Indians at Grand Portage* by
Eastman Johnson, Permanent Collection, St. Louis County Historical Society, Duluth, MN;
pp. 156-157—*Canoe of Indians* by Eastman Johnson (detail), Permanent Collection, St. Louis
County Historical Society; wigwams, State Historical Society of Wisconsin, Madison,
neg. #WHi (X3) 34131 ; fur-trade engraving by Claude Joseph Sauthier (detail), National
Archives of Canada, Ottawa, #C-007300; teakettle, earbobs, and beads, Minnesota
Historical Society, St. Paul; beaver pelt, State Historical Society of Wisconsin Museum;
pp. 158-159—ledger pages, State Historical Society of Wisconsin, Wisconsin Fur Trade Accounts,
Vol. 1; map by Susan McAliley; copy of *Shooting the Rapids* by Frances Anne Hopkins (detail),
National Archives of Canada, #C-0016425; paddle, Museum Collections, Minnesota Historical
Society; rendezvous painting © Howard Sivertson from *The Illustrated Voyageur,* published by
Lake Superior Port Cities Inc., Duluth, MN; pp. 160-161—Métis woman, State Historical
Society of Wisconsin, neg. #Whi (X3) 24634; doll, State Historical Society of Wisconsin,
neg. #1955.453; quilled moccasin, private collection; beaded moccasin and beaver engraving,
Minnesota Historical Society; Ojibwe girls, courtesy Catherine Whipple.

Cover and Map Illustrations: Jean-Paul Tibbles
Line Art: Greg Dearth
Editorial Direction: Peg Ross
Art Direction: Jane Varda
Design: Laura Moberly and Justin Packard

Library of Congress Cataloging-in-Publication Data
Ernst, Kathleen, 1959-
Trouble at Fort La Pointe / by Kathleen Ernst. — 1st ed.
p. cm. — (History mysteries ; 7)
"American girl."
Summary: In the early 1700s, twelve-year-old Suzette, an Ojibwa-French girl,
hopes that her father will win the fur-trapping contest so that he can quit being a
voyageur and stay with his family year-round, but when he is accused of stealing, Suzette
must use her knowledge of both French and Ojibwa ways to find the real thief.

ISBN 1-58485-087-6 — ISBN 1-58485-086-8 (pbk.)
1. Ojibwa Indians—Superior, Lake, Region—Juvenile fiction. [1. Ojibwa Indians—
Superior, Lake, Region—Fiction. 2. Indians of North America—Superior, Lake, Region—
Fiction. 3. Fur traders—Fiction. 4. Racially mixed people—Fiction. 5. Superior, Lake,
Region—Fiction. 6. Mystery and detective stories.]
I. Title. II. Series.
PZ7.E732 Tr 2000   [Fic]—dc21   00-020020

*To the many people who helped me
peek back to the fur-trade era, including
Linda Albers, Lac du Flambeau, Wisconsin;
Robert Powless and Dana Jackson, Odanah, Wisconsin;
Steve Cotherman, Madeline Island, Wisconsin;
Steve Brisson, Michilimackinac, Michigan;
and the interpreters at Old Fort William,
Thunder Bay, Ontario.*

Miigwech! Merci! Thank you!

TABLE OF CONTENTS

Chapter I
To the Island

Maybe today, Suzette thought hopefully as she slipped on her moccasins. *Maybe today our family can paddle to the island!* After days of stormy weather, sweet new-morning sun sifted through the pine and birch trees surrounding the Ojibwe camp. She'd find Papa and ask him.

Leaving the *wiigwams* and cook fires behind, she hurried along a faint path that led through the woods to the lakeshore. At water's edge, she paused to look out over the sparkling lake. La Pointe Island beckoned in the distance. Fort La Pointe, the fur-trading post, seemed tiny as a child's toy, the French flag flying above it no more than a spot of color. Squinting, Suzette could almost make out the Ojibwe lodges that already dotted the field beside the fort.

The lake was so big that the French traders called it *Lac Supérieur*—Lake Superior. Different bands of the great Ojibwe tribe lived all around the lake, much farther than

Suzette had ever traveled. In rough weather, waves could capsize even the largest birch-bark canoe. But this morning, the lake looked welcoming, and the sky was a cloudless blue. "As blue as your beautiful eyes," Papa often said on such mornings. Suzette smiled. The echo of his voice reached inside like a ray of spring sunshine.

She took a deep breath, enjoying the damp smell of earth, the lapping of the waves, and the sun warming her shoulders like a trader's wool blanket. Still smiling, Suzette glanced back at the camp. Smoke from morning fires twisted toward the sky, and the first shouts of children at play mixed with the mournful yipping of hungry dogs. It was good to be among more *wiigwams* again!

Ojibwe people moved with the seasons. During the cold winter months, when food was scarce, they scattered into the deep forest in small family camps. At the end of the long winter, it felt wonderful to move on to the sugaring camp, where perhaps a dozen families gathered to tap maple trees for sap to boil into syrup and sugar. And then Ojibwe people all over the mainland began making their way to the great summer village on La Pointe Island, just like Suzette's family. Each day now, more families arrived at the campground along the lakeshore and pitched *wiigwams* among the trees, waiting for good weather so they could cross to the island. Every passing day brought happy reunions with friends and relatives Suzette hadn't seen since last summer.

And soon would come the greatest reunion of all! Suzette gazed across the dancing water to La Pointe Island again, almost bouncing with excitement. She had spent every summer of her life on the island that the Ojibwe called *Moningwanekaaning.* It had been the summer gathering place of the Ojibwe people for generations, long before the French arrived. Suzette loved the island more than any place she knew. During the busy summer months, La Pointe was home to many people: Ojibwe families and French traders, soldiers, and canoe men. Sometimes Ho Chunk or Menominee or Potawatomie trappers, who lived many days' travel from La Pointe, paddled their furs to the trading post. Once a trapper with skin black as night had spent two days on the island. It was a big, noisy mix of people. Suzette couldn't imagine passing through the seasons' circle without summering outside the walls of Fort La Pointe.

And this year, because of the trappers' competition, her family would have even more to celebrate. This year—

"Suzette!"

Suzette grinned and waved when she saw Gabrielle Broussard emerge from the trees, carrying a copper kettle. Gabrielle was her best friend. They had both been born in the moon of blooming flowers, twelve years earlier. And they both had French fathers.

"*Aaniin,*" Gabrielle greeted her. "What are you doing?"

"I'm going to find Papa. He walked out to the point, to get the best view of the lake. Want to come with me?"

Gabrielle splashed into the water to fill the kettle. "Mama's waiting for me. What's your papa doing there?"

"Can't you guess? He's watching for the *voyageurs*!" Suzette's feet scuffed the earth in a little dance. Any day now, the songs of the French *voyageurs* would ring across the water from the east. They were paddling huge canoes filled with trade goods from a far-off place called Montréal. The trip took many weeks, down mighty rivers and across two great lakes. Their arrival on La Pointe Island would spark the wildly joyous gathering called *rendez-vous* by the French and *maawanji'iwin* by the Ojibwe. By the end of the short summer visit, the *voyageurs'* canoes would be loaded with the furs the Ojibwe trappers had been collecting all year. Then the *voyageurs* would say their good-byes and paddle back to Montréal before snowstorms and iced-over rivers made travel impossible.

"Papa can't wait to see his old friends again," Suzette added. Her own papa had been a *voyageur* for many years.

Gabrielle glanced to the east, her face wistful. "I'm waiting too."

Suzette stopped dancing. For a moment she had forgotten that Gabrielle's father would be among the paddlers. Gabrielle hadn't seen her father since the moon of shining leaves, when the woods blazed with red and yellow and the air held a promise of coming snow. Suzette chewed her lip. "I'm sure your papa will arrive soon, Gabrielle. I'm sure his journeys have been safe."

Gabrielle nodded, but she didn't smile.

What would cheer up her friend? "I'm hoping Papa will say we can cross to the island today!" she confided.

"Ooh, maybe we can cross today too!" Gabrielle said hopefully, then cocked her head toward the camp. "Mama's calling me. I have to go."

I'm glad I'm not waiting for Papa to arrive this year, Suzette thought as she walked down the path toward the rocky finger of land jutting into the lake. For most of Suzette's life, she too had anxiously waited for her papa to arrive with the *voyageurs* each spring. She knew what that felt like. Every year one or two of the *voyageurs* who had Ojibwe families left and didn't come back, sending word that they had no wish to leave Montréal again. Sometimes *voyageurs* drowned or got injured when canoes capsized in storms or hit rocks and broke up in river rapids. Suzette's own grandfather, Grandmother's first husband, had died along that journey while Mama was still a baby. A winter spent waiting and wondering was hard to endure. Suzette didn't ever want to feel that way again.

She hurried down the trail, enjoying the sparkle of water visible through the trees and the soft feel of pine needles blanketing the ground. She caught sight of Papa sitting on a rock, staring out over the water. His whittling knife and a sharpened stick lay beside him.

Suzette paused at the edge of the woods, looking at the familiar figure: red hair and beard, very broad shoulders,

strong hands now oddly still. She glanced toward the eastern horizon. Two black cormorants skimmed above the
lake. There was nothing else to see. No canoes.

She looked back at her father. It was strange to see
Philippe Choudoir sitting quietly. "Papa!"

Papa turned, and a huge grin lit his face. "Suzette!
Have you come to keep your papa company, *mignonne?*"
He engulfed her in a big hug as she dropped onto the
rock beside him.

"*Oui,*" Suzette said in his native French. They spoke
Ojibwe with the rest of the family, but she and Papa
always spoke French when they were alone, so she could
practice. "Any sign of the *voyageurs* yet?"

"*Non,* not yet. But any day now." Papa rummaged in
his pocket for his old clay pipe and pouch of tobacco.

"You've missed your friends, haven't you." She'd known
it during the long cold months of their first winter together.
Around the fire at night, when the Ojibwe men told stories
of bear hunts or falling through thin ice or other adven-
tures, Papa told tales of his canoe days, with a faraway look
in his eyes.

Papa lit his pipe and regarded her. "*Oui.* I miss my
friends. But not as much as I missed my family, all those
years I traveled with the canoe men. I am very happy
I made the choice to stay here with you last fall."

His words made Suzette feel warm inside. "Well,
soon you will see your friends again." She was as eager

for the *voyageurs'* arrival as he was. "It will be a grand reunion, *non?*"

Papa grinned. "A grand reunion! A celebration!"

"And once the *voyageurs* arrive, Captain d'Amboise will end the competition! And surely you'll win the prize!" Captain d'Amboise was in charge of Fort La Pointe, on the island. The trappers' competition had been his idea.

"Shhh!" Papa warned, looking around.

"There's no one about to hear!"

"Only your Spirit of the Woods, perhaps," Papa said seriously. "Or the Spirit of the Waves."

Papa tried to be respectful of Ojibwe ways. The Ojibwe believed in *Gizhe Manido,* the Great Spirit, but they also knew that all things had a spirit. Papa had just one spirit, God, to protect him. He carried a small silver crucifix on a band of blue, red, and yellow that Mama had woven in a lightning pattern, and he had once given Suzette a little silver cross of her own. But he believed that Suzette, as a *Métis* girl of mixed blood, had *both* kinds of spirits to protect her.

She hoped he was right. She found the thought comforting. "We'll keep our secret," she whispered. "But, Papa, I know you're going to win. You have to! Surely no one trapped more beaver than you last winter! And mink, and otter, and—" She sputtered into silence, remembering how Papa had run his traps every day during the coldest months, ranging far from their winter lodge on snowshoes and returning with ice crusted in his beard. Papa hated trapping. But he had done it.

"We all worked hard," Papa agreed. "You and your mother and grandmother helped by cleaning so many furs. And the rabbits and foxes you caught in your snares will count too." His eyes danced. "I think it just may be enough. If I win the competition for having the most furs, you won't have to work so hard next winter, Suzette. I can use the prize money to pay my debt to the fur trade company."

Suzette nodded. Papa's debt was like a heavy load the family had been hauling on their sleds all winter. By choosing to stay with his family year-round, Papa had broken his contract with the fur-trade company that had hired him to work as a *voyageur.* Some *voyageurs* who liked Ojibwe life simply broke their contracts and stayed, far from the reach of French authorities. But Papa said he wouldn't be able to sleep at night if he did such a thing.

Instead, Captain d'Amboise had sent a letter to the company on Papa's behalf, asking that he be granted one year to pay his debt. If Papa won the competition and used the prize to pay his debt, he would be free to stay with his family forever. If he didn't win the competition, he would have to return to Montréal with the other *voyageurs* at the end of the summer trading season.

"I believe you're going to win," Suzette said again, hoping that saying it over and over would make it come true. Suddenly she caught her breath. "Papa! I almost forgot. Mama and Grandmother have fixed a kettle of wild rice and maple sugar. And Yellow Wing trapped some whitefish." Yellow Wing was Mama's brother.

"Well, I don't want to keep your mama waiting." Papa took one last look to the east, then pushed to his feet.

"Papa . . . I can't wait to get to the island and set up our summer camp. Do you think we'll be crossing today? The water seems calm, doesn't it? I think it's safe enough." Suzette held her breath.

Papa laughed. "So you know more about this lake than your *voyageur* papa, eh?"

Suzette felt her face grow warm. It was surely her French blood that sometimes made her speak disrespect-fully to her elders! "No, Papa, but—"

"No matter. You know I like you to speak your mind." He ruffled her hair with his hand. "I need to speak with Yellow Wing."

"And Grandmother," Suzette reminded him. In French families, men made most of the important decisions. It was different among Ojibwe people, and sometimes Papa still forgot to ask Grandmother's opinions. Grandmother's second husband, an Ojibwe man, had died two years earlier. But Grandmother was still strong.

"And Grandmother."

They walked back to the camp together and threaded through the *wiigwams* scattered among the trees near the shore. Suzette smiled, enjoying the shrieks of children playing, the Ojibwe man who stopped Papa to tell him a funny story, the smell of beaver tail boiling over a neighbor's cook fire, the nods and greetings awaiting her at every turn.

They found the morning meal simmering over the cook fire in front of their lodge. Papa put his arm around Mama's waist. "Your daughter believes that today is a good day to cross to the island," he said in Ojibwe.

Suzette watched hopefully. They made a handsome couple. Although Mama was half French, she looked just like Grandmother. She was slender, and she wore her black hair neatly braided. With her deerskin dress and leggings, she wore huge silver earrings that Papa had given her, and many necklaces. Papa was shorter than his wife but strong as a black bear. He wore a striped cotton shirt, a red sash around his waist, and the tall top hat he'd worn during his *voyageur* days, but also Ojibwe moccasins and leather leggings.

Mama laughed, then turned to her own mother. "Grandmother? What do you think?"

Grandmother nodded. "I had already decided that this would be a good day to move to our summer camp."

"Yiyiyiyiyi!" Suzette yelped happily. They were going to La Pointe!

As soon as everyone had eaten, the family began
to pack for the move. Mama put Suzette's baby sister
Charlotte in her cradleboard and hung it from a tree,
where she could watch and hear the family. Suzette helped
her mother and grandmother take apart their two lodges.
At this temporary campsite, the family had sheltered in
quickly built cone-shaped lodges framed with spruce poles
tied together at the top. Grandmother, Mama, and Suzette
left the poles in place but carefully removed the coverings,
made of large pieces of birch bark and woven reed mats,
which they would need on the island.

Papa didn't like to see Mama and Grandmother haul
heavy burdens, so he and Yellow Wing carried the family's
belongings to the lakeshore. Suzette helped with the
lighter baskets and bags but left the weighty bundles
of furs for the men. During the past winter, Papa and
Yellow Wing had made two trips across the frozen lake
to take furs to the trading post on La Pointe. But they
still had many more.

Surely enough furs to win the competition! Suzette thought
happily, as she carried a basket filled with pouches of dried
berries and herbs to the beach. Excited, she couldn't help
swinging the basket in a big arc—

"Yeh!" someone grunted, just as Suzette felt the basket
thump against something.

She turned to see a man on the path just behind her,
heading toward the lakeshore with a canoe carefully

balanced over his head. She had hit the bow of the canoe
with her basket. "I'm sorry," she said humbly, taking a
step backward.

Although his head was almost hidden beneath the
canoe, Suzette recognized a man named Niskigwun. His
son Two Fish was walking behind the canoe.

Suzette didn't know Niskigwun and Two Fish well,
but during the moon of crusted snow, they had happened
across her family's camp and taken lodging for the night.
Niskigwun's wife was dead, and he and his son were traveling alone. Two Fish, who was about Suzette's age, was a
disagreeable, stick-thin boy with a broken front tooth.
Niskigwun had spent most of the evening bragging about
the number of beaver pelts he had to trade at La Pointe.

"Careless girl," Niskigwun growled as he passed.
"You'd be wise to pay more attention."

"I said *pardonnez-moi*," Suzette muttered.

She didn't think it was loud enough to be heard, but
Two Fish stopped and glared. "What did you say?" he
hissed. "Your fancy French talk isn't welcome here,
Blue Eyes. *Blue Eyes!* You are an ugly girl. I'm glad you're
not my sister. I'd be ashamed." Then he hurried after
his father.

For a moment Suzette stared after him, her mouth
open. She knew that all of the other *Métis* people she'd
ever seen—Mama and Gabrielle and a handful of others—
looked Ojibwe. None of the other *Métis* people had blue

eyes. But no one had ever insulted her for her unusual appearance before.

What a rude boy! No wonder Two Fish didn't have many friends. Still, Suzette had to admit the exchange was partly her fault. If she'd been paying attention, and if she'd held her tongue—

"I didn't expect to see you daydreaming today!"

Suzette jumped. She hadn't noticed Papa approaching, heading back for another load.

Papa leaned close. "Maybe you're picturing your papa winning the competition, eh?"

"*Oui.*" His enthusiasm made Suzette feel good. What did it matter what an annoying boy like Two Fish said? The air was fragrant with tobacco smoke and pine. At the campsite, her mother had been humming. Even Grandmother seemed to move lightly, as if the sun had driven winter's stiffness from her bones. They were going to La Pointe!

And . . . the end of the trappers' competition was in sight!

CHAPTER 2

INTO THE LAKE

Many friends came to the lakefront to see Suzette's family off. "We'll be crossing today too!" Gabrielle told Suzette. "We're just not packed up yet."

"I can tell Papa is eager," Suzette laughed. "He's moving fast!"

Papa splashed into the water, a heavy bundle of furs balanced with long-practiced ease on his shoulder. If he minded the biting cold water, he showed no sign. "This is the last one, Suzette," he called. "Ready to go?"

The family owned two large birch-bark canoes for transporting themselves and their belongings, and a smaller one Suzette used for short trips along the shoreline. The three canoes were staked and floating in hip-deep water offshore to protect their fragile seams from rocks. Papa didn't permit Suzette to paddle across the open waters of the great lake, so he and Yellow Wing packed her canoe full and tied it behind one of the larger ones. Suzette and

Mama waded out and settled Charlotte in place before gently climbing into Papa's canoe. Grandmother paddled in the bow, or front, of Yellow Wing's canoe.

"We'll see you on the island!" Suzette yelled, waving hard. Then Papa and Yellow Wing dipped their paddles for the first powerful strokes.

Suzette sat in the center of Papa's canoe, wedged among their belongings. She kept an eye on Charlotte, whose cradleboard was braced against a crossbar. Mama paddled in the bow and Papa in the rear. Leaning back against a bundle of furs, Suzette dabbled her fingers in the water. A pair of merganser ducks paddled nearby, then dove, chasing fish below the surface. Papa was already singing one of his favorite paddling songs.

Soon the shore of the mainland faded behind them. Content, Suzette barely noticed when she felt a trickle of cold water in the bottom of the canoe. She reached for a piece of heavy cotton cloth kept as protection against leaks and sopped up the water. But before she could wring out the cloth, the trickle became a stream. "Papa! We're taking water."

"Mop it up the best you can. It can't be serious. Yellow Wing and I sealed every seam with fresh pitch yesterday." Papa began to sing again.

At first Suzette wasn't worried either. Wasn't Papa one of the best canoe men on the great lake? He and Yellow Wing knew how to tend canoes. But water was soon appearing faster than she could soak it up. She scrambled to find a small birch-bark *makak* and began to bail.

Papa stopped singing. "I've got water back here now. What is this?" He sounded puzzled.

Mama turned around. "My feet are wet too, Philippe. Shall I stop paddling and help bail?"

"No." Papa's blue eyes narrowed with worry. "We're a long way from either shore. We need to paddle hard. Suzette, keep bailing."

"I'm trying!" It was difficult, though, because the canoe was packed so full that there was little room to scoop the *makak*. Suzette felt the cold water around her thighs. A shiver chased away the sun's warmth. They were in the middle of the passage now, about evenly distant from the mainland and the island. Too far to swim in the icy water. Too far to shout for help. The loaded canoes were riding low in the water already, and water was rushing in faster than she could get rid of it.

They were in trouble.

Yellow Wing eased his canoe close, frowning. "What's this? That canoe was sound yesterday."

"I don't know, but we're taking water. Come closer." Papa stopped paddling and grabbed the other canoe. "Suzette, pass Charlotte over to your grandmother."

A finger of fear, icy as the lake, crooked around Suzette's heart when she looked at her baby sister. Charlotte was asleep, shaded from the sun by a woven mat. Suzette gingerly lifted the cradleboard and passed it to her grand-mother's waiting arms.

"Papa, shall I try to cross over too?" Suzette asked. "Or pass over some of our belongings to lighten our load?"

"No. The other canoe is too full to take any more weight. And I need you to bail." Papa leaned into his paddle. The powerful muscles he'd developed during his *voyageur* days rippled beneath his shirt. Every stroke sent the canoe surging ahead.

The water had risen to fist-deep. Suzette reached for the bailer again, feeling another shiver of fear down her spine.

"Don't worry, *mignonne*," Papa called. "If we must, we will throw a bundle or two of furs overboard. That will lighten our load."

"Papa, *no!*" Papa needed to turn in every one of his furs at the trading post. If they discarded furs, he would surely lose the competition!

The fun of *rendez-vous* was forgotten. Mama and Papa's hard paddling seemed to bring them no closer to La Pointe. Despite Suzette's bailing, water rose two fists deep inside the canoe. Cold water bit through her leggings.

Whenever she dared, Suzette snatched a glance toward the island. The fort danced teasingly in the distance. Water rose three fists high.

Soon every muscle in Suzette's body ached, drawn tight as a bowstring with worry and the effort of desperate bailing. She felt sick as she watched water rise to within two fists of the canoe's top edge.

Finally Mama stopped paddling and turned her head, careful not to upset their balance. "Philippe, we mustn't swamp. We will lose everything."

The brief silence was painful. Suzette heard a gull calling and looked again toward shore. It was still too far. They could not reach shore without lightening their load. And the water was so deep that if they threw their belongings overboard, the blankets and kettles and tools they needed to survive could not be retrieved.

Papa put his paddle down. "I'm going to toss over some furs." His voice was tight. Suzette watched him struggle to loosen a bulky bundle of stiff furs from the tightly packed canoe. *No!* She wanted to weep. All her hopes for the future were about to be cast overboard.

Suzette didn't think. Instead came the sudden slam of cold, burning her skin, stealing her breath, as she eased her feet over the canoe and slipped into the water. It took all her effort to grasp the canoe before the lake claimed her.

"*Suzette!*" Papa bellowed. The canoe was rocking dangerously. He steadied it even as his huge fist clamped around her wrist like iron. "What are you doing?" He began to pull her from the water.

"Papa, pa-paddle!" Suzette begged, her teeth chattering. "Please d-don't lose any furs." She wanted to say more, but the lake was squeezing her chest, locking out the words.

"Philippe, pull her in!" Mama cried. Her voice could have cracked ice.

Suzette heard her mother's fear and found the strength to speak once more. "*Paddle!*" she gasped. "I can hold on."

She heard a paddle splash behind her. "Philippe, keep going," Yellow Wing echoed urgently. "I'll stay beside Suzette. If she slips, I'll grab her. Now go!"

Suzette moved hand-over-hand until her weight was balanced behind the canoe. She clenched her fingers around the cedar frame. Her legs felt like logs, too stiff to kick. She closed her eyes and concentrated on holding on. A few moments later she heard Papa bellow again, then distant shouts. "Help is coming, Suzette," Papa called. "Don't let go."

She didn't know how long she was pulled through the water. The numbing cold robbed her fingers of sensation. She couldn't hold on any longer. *Yellow Wing!* she tried to call, but the words wouldn't come. And when she felt strong arms lift her from the aching cold, she wasn't sure if she'd been rescued or if one of the spirits, Papa's God or Mama's Spirit of the Waves, had claimed her for their own.

CHAPTER 3
SABOTAGE

No fire's warmth had ever felt so good. Not on the most bitter winter day, when her breath clouded in the brittle air and she had to snowshoe through chest-high drifts to check her snares. Not even the time she had fallen through the ice into a stream, and her leggings had frozen so stiff she'd had to drag herself home. Suzette lifted her face to the sun, hugged the wool blanket more tightly around her shoulders, and edged closer to the flames. She was huddled on the sandy beach below Fort La Pointe.

"*Miigwech, miigwech,*" her parents were saying in thanks to the two Ojibwe men who'd seen their trouble and paddled out to pull Suzette from the lake. "*Miigwech,*" Suzette echoed, but it came out a whisper, and she wasn't sure they'd heard. Mama pressed gifts of appreciation— a fishing lure, a pipe—into their hands. Then Papa said a prayer, fingering his silver cross, and Grandmother offered tobacco to the lake in thanks for their safe passage.

When the two men had gone, Papa gave Suzette one last, crushing hug before turning back to the canoes. Grandmother began to brew some tea of wintergreen leaves and wild cherry twigs. Mama knelt by Suzette, stroking her hair. "Daughter, you were foolish," she scolded softly. "Haven't we taught you better?"

"But, Mama, Papa was going to lose a bundle of furs! All our work! It would mean—"

"Hush. I know what it would mean. Do you think anything means more than your safety?"

"I didn't mean to scare you," Suzette mumbled. The crackling fire and pungent smell of burning pine were lulling her to sleep. "I just knew we couldn't let Papa throw away his furs. It would have ruined everything . . ."

"Stop talking and drink," Grandmother ordered, pouring a bowl of steaming tea. The women watched until she had finished, then coaxed her down on a blanket. "Rest," they murmured, and Suzette was happy to obey.

Drowsily, Suzette watched the men unload the canoes and pile the family's belongings near the fire. Charlotte fretted and Mama soothed her back to sleep with an Ojibwe lullaby. Suzette was just drifting to sleep when Papa's voice, sharp as a skinning knife, cut through her sleepy haze. "Someone did this."

Suzette opened her eyes. Papa and Yellow Wing were

squatting beside Papa's canoe, now empty and resting upside down on the beach nearby.

"That's not possible." Yellow Wing bent close.

Papa's face was as red as his hair. "What else can it be? That seam was solid last night. You and I both inspected every seam in this canoe."

Suzette knew it was true. She had watched Papa and Yellow Wing prepare the canoes for the crossing. They had restitched several fragile seams in the birch bark with *watab,* split spruce root threaded through holes made with sharp awls. Then they had carefully sealed cracks with pine pitch. Papa and Yellow Wing knew their canoes like they knew their family.

"Look at this seam." Papa pointed. "Most of the pitch was scraped away. If all of it had been removed, I would have seen immediately. But just enough was taken to let us get out in deep water."

"*Philippe!*" Mama breathed. She caught Papa's eye, then glanced at Suzette as if to say, *Don't frighten your daughter.* Suzette narrowed her eyes to slits, wanting to hear more.

After a moment Yellow Wing said in a low voice, "Someone was trying to harm you or the family?"

"Perhaps just scare me." Through the veil of her lashes, Suzette saw Papa's eyes spark like flint on a fire steel.

"But who . . ." Yellow Wing let the sentence die as he glanced toward Mama. She shook her head. Grandmother's lips were pinched together.

"I don't know," Papa said grimly. "But I would like to find out." He pushed to his feet. "Come on. Let's get these things moved up to the woods. I want to make camp."

Suzette abandoned her pretense of sleeping and sat up, hugging the blanket close around her shoulders. Papa's discovery was chilling as spring snow. A man's canoe was among his most precious—and necessary—possessions. Each was painted with a unique design. Papa had painted a leaping fish on the bow of his. Everyone knew who it belonged to.

Perhaps he's mistaken, she thought. *He must be.* No one had reason to wish Papa—or his family—any harm.

Did they?

The family began their first trip from the beach up to the campground in brooding silence. Trying to push her troublesome thoughts away, Suzette drew a deep breath and took in the familiar sights of La Pointe.

The French trading post sat on the southwestern shore, just above the beach, in a big grassy meadow. A tall log stockade surrounded the post. Suzette noticed that a few logs had been replaced recently, giving the walls a funny striped look. Hundreds of *wiigwams* already dotted the meadow by the fort. In a small field that had been scraped from the earth nearby, Suzette could see Ojibwe women planting potatoes, corn, and squash. As Suzette's family made their way through the campground, friends called to them from all sides.

The family returned to their usual place beneath pines at the meadow's edge, marked by lodgepoles they'd left planted in the ground the year before. "The framework is still good," Grandmother announced, examining the poles, which were bent and tied with basswood twine to form arches. Since the family would be here all summer, they had two *wiigwams,* or lodges: one for Mama, Papa, Suzette, and Charlotte, the other for Grandmother and Yellow Wing.

Suzette helped cover the top of the dome-shaped frames with birch bark. She stood on tiptoe to hold the pieces in place while Grandmother and Mama lashed them to the poles. Next they unrolled lengths of bulrush mats to cover the sides. They arranged the mats to allow breezes inside during hot days, and left a smoke hole in the roof so they could have a cook fire inside on rainy ones.

Suzette inhaled the scent of fresh cedar boughs as she spread them on the ground inside and covered them with rush mats. In her own corner, she neatly folded her sleeping blankets and deer hides tanned with the hair on them. Tidying the lodge and making it snug against the weather usually made her feel safe. At home.

But today was different. No matter how hard she tried, she couldn't forget Papa's words. *Someone did this* . . . They circled in her head like a buzzing black fly.

Papa must have noticed her mood, because once his chores were done, he poked his head into the lodge and beckoned. "Come, Suzette, I want to take some furs to the post. Shall we go find your old friend Monsieur Roussain? And see about your summer lessons?"

Suzette scrambled to her feet and joined him outside. "Oh, *oui,* Papa! Yes!" She was eager to visit the clerk who gave her French lessons.

Grandmother, who was arranging the area between their *wiigwams* where she would build the cook fire, shook her head. "Philippe, your daughter should spend her time learning how to make some Ojibwe man a good wife one day."

Papa put an arm around Grandmother's shoulders. "But, Grandmother, with such a teacher as you, how could Suzette not be well prepared?"

Grandmother shook her head again, but she couldn't hide her smile.

Papa hoisted a bundle of furs onto his shoulder, and he and Suzette set off across the meadow toward the stockade. "I want to get most of my furs safe in the trading post and marked in the ledger," he whispered to Suzette. "But I've hidden a few bundles in the woods. Captain d'Amboise won't close the competition until the *voyageurs* arrive. I'll bring my hidden furs in at the last minute, eh? I don't want anyone to know how many furs Philippe Choudoir has for the competition."

"Monsieur Roussain will be impressed by the quality of your furs, I know. And I'll be glad to see him again."

Papa smiled. "I'm glad you enjoy your French lessons. I'll arrange lessons for Charlotte, too, when she's old enough."

"Papa . . . why don't other *voyageurs* teach their children to read and write?"

Papa paused to better balance the load he was carrying. "Well, most of my *voyageur* friends come from poor families. They can barely read and write themselves. But since my father was a merchant in Montréal, he could afford to send me to school. That's why I know how important reading and writing can be."

Suzette frowned, trying to understand.

"It's hard to explain, *mignonne*." Papa sighed. "Life is very different in Montréal. Ojibwe people are respected if they give away their possessions to people in need. But where I come from, the most important people are those who hold on to their money and possessions."

Suzette felt baffled. What kind of place was this, where selfishness was honored?

Papa shook his head. Then he grinned, his blue eyes dancing. "Well, rich or not, your papa was too restless to study. I ran away from school, and from Montréal too, eh? So I could become a *voyageur* and marry your mama!"

He was still chuckling as they reached the rough log walls of the stockade. As they passed through the gate,

Suzette looked around eagerly. Papa said Fort La Pointe was a small outpost compared to some of the other trading posts, but it still seemed grand to Suzette.

"Look, Papa, they've built the carpenter a larger shop!" she exclaimed. They paused for a moment, looking for other changes, but the other post buildings were just as she remembered. One long, low building included the store and attached storage room, the carpentry shop, and a workshop with a small blacksmith's anvil. Facing those were quarters for Captain d'Amboise and Monsieur Roussain. The French soldiers stationed at La Pointe, and the French laborers who hauled heavy loads and kept the fort in good repair, slept in crowded rooms beyond. The buildings were all made of vertical logs pounded into the ground like tree trunks, their slanted roofs covered with strips of cedar bark.

"It must be very strange to live in buildings like that," Suzette mused, thinking of their cozy lodges. What would it be like to live within such solid walls? Would she still be able to smell a coming rain? Hear the ice begin to drip in the night during the first spring thaw? Add wood to the fire without leaving the warmth of her sleeping robes? "I don't think I'd like it."

"I'm happier in our *wiigwam* too." Papa smiled. "Come on."

They found Monsieur Roussain, the post clerk, in the store. The small room smelled of tobacco and wood smoke.

Monsieur Roussain was working at the counter. Ceiling-high shelves lined all four walls. Suzette saw at once how few goods—cloth for new shirts, iron kettles, pretty silver earbobs—were left on the shelves. Monsieur Roussain was probably as eager for the *voyageurs'* arrival as Papa.

"Ah, Philippe!" the clerk grinned, pushing aside a ledger as they came inside. "And my friend Suzette! *Comment allez-vous?* How are you?"

"*Très bien, merci,*" she responded. "I am very well, thank you." She pinched the sides of her deerskin dress and bobbed up and down in something called a curtsy, as he had taught her.

Papa dumped his stiff furs on the counter. "Here are more furs for my account. The finest, of course! But I also wanted to make arrangements for Suzette's lessons."

Monsieur Roussain was a thin man, very tall. He sat down on his stool so he didn't tower over them. "We can start this afternoon, if you'd like." The clerk smiled at Suzette, then looked back to Papa with a twinkle in his eye. "Although, Philippe, your friends will probably tease you again for this."

"I want the best for Suzette," Papa said simply. "I think more French people will be coming to this country. Being able to read and write the language can only help her. Even if she is a girl."

Suzette didn't care why Papa did this for her, she was just glad that he did. Reading amazed her. To think that someone she had never met could make tiny marks on a piece of paper, and she could know what he had been thinking!

Papa couldn't afford to pay Monsieur Roussain, so the two men worked out a trade: fresh fish delivered weekly, and a new pair of moccasins that Mama had volunteered to make, in exchange for the lessons. "I'll be back with more furs," Papa promised Roussain before he left. "And make sure these get credited to the right account, eh?"

"I've got Suzette here to keep me straight," Roussain laughed. "Suzette, do you want to record your papa's furs? Come back behind the counter."

Roussain often had her practice writing and arithmetic by helping keep his ledgers. They were huge, leather-bound account books brought all the way from Montréal. Suzette opened a ledger on the counter and carefully leafed through until she found the page where Monsieur Roussain had written *PHILIPPE CHOUDOIR* across the top. Each visit Papa had made to the trading post was noted on the page: the date, how many pelts he'd brought, and what supplies he'd taken. He already had many pelts to his credit.

Holding her breath, she carefully dipped the clerk's quill pen in the inkpot and listed the six beaver pelts that Papa had just brought. Her writing was not nearly as fine as Monsieur Roussain's. But it was exciting to add to Papa's list!

The clerk smiled. "Very good, Suzette! I'll just toss these furs into the storage room. Now that the weather's finally cleared and more people are crossing, I've got lots of pelts coming in."

Roussain opened a door behind the counter, and the musky odor of raw pelts spilled into the store. He stepped inside the narrow room where he stored the furs. Standing in the doorway, Suzette watched him drop Papa's beaver pelts onto a waist-high pile. In the middle of the room, two laborers were busy packing some of the loose furs into huge bales. *Voyageurs* would paddle the bales back to warehouses in faraway Montréal. Suzette shivered with excitement. Soon they would be packing Papa's furs into bales! Who would wear the hats made from Papa's beaver pelts? Those distant strangers would never know that these very furs had helped Philippe Choudoir win a trappers' competition!

Suzette spent the afternoon in the store with the clerk, then wandered back to her lodge. More families had arrived from the mainland. All through the camp, Suzette could see cook fires burning. Some boys had started a noisy round of the game called *bagaadowe* by the Ojibwe and *la crosse* by the French.

At home she found Grandmother boiling wild rice

in an iron kettle over the fire. Mama was tending several fish roasting on sharpened sticks near the flames. Papa, Yellow Wing, and some friends were playing a game nearby, trying to guess whether partly scorched sticks would fall right-side-up when tossed. Charlotte watched from her cradleboard, propped against a log.

Suzette tried to convince herself that everything was as it should be, but she still heard the echoes of Papa's words as he bent over the damaged canoe that morning: *Someone did this.* Who would want to hurt her family? Who could have done such a thing?

That night, long after settling on her sleeping blankets, she heard Papa and Mama creep from the lodge. Through the bulrush matting that formed the walls of the *wiigwam,* she could see light glimmering as they blew the fire back to life. A moment later she caught a faint whiff of tobacco. Papa had lit his pipe. Suzette pulled herself up on one elbow. She could just barely hear her mother speak.

"It's late," Mama murmured. "You should sleep."

"I can't."

A silence. Then, "You're worried about the canoe."

"Of course I am!" Papa burst out, then lowered his voice. "How can I not be? My family was put in danger! Suzette could have drowned." In the long pause that followed, Suzette pictured her father puffing on his pipe, staring at the embers of their fire.

"She did it for you, Philippe," Mama said. "She's afraid you'll have to leave us."

"I may have to paddle back to Montréal in the fall," he said slowly. "But I'll be back in the spring, Shining Stone. I will always come back."

There was another pause. "Some French men don't," Mama said finally. "You know it as well as I. And so does Suzette."

Suzette felt suddenly cold, and she burrowed beneath her warm blankets and furs, wishing her parents would stop talking and come inside.

"*I* will *always* come back." Papa's voice was hushed but firm. "I have no wish to go back to Montréal. And I am too stubborn to get sick or hurt on the journey, eh?"

Mama murmured something Suzette couldn't hear.

"Oh, Shining Stone . . ." Suddenly Papa sounded weary. "The last thing I wanted was to bring sadness to those I love. I know your mother wanted you to marry an Ojibwe man . . ."

Grandmother had advised Mama not to marry Papa? Suzette had never heard that before. She wished she hadn't heard it now. As she stared at the shadows flickering on the birch bark above her, a chill began to gather in the pit of her stomach.

CHAPTER 4
THE CAPTAIN'S ANNOUNCEMENT

 The sunrise brought a beautiful day to La Pointe Island. A light breeze skittered through the camp, and sunlight danced on the lake. Suzette stayed near the lodge with her mother and grandmother. A stream of old friends— including Gabrielle—stopped by. Mama and Grandmother seemed happy, but Suzette couldn't shake away thoughts of everything that had happened since they left the mainland.

Finally she felt so restless that she was sure she couldn't sit still one more moment. "Mama, may I go find Papa?" she asked, setting aside the moccasins she'd been stitching. "I think he went to watch for the *voyageurs*."

"A'jawac," Grandmother said. She used Suzette's Ojibwe name, which meant "carried safely over the water." Soon after Suzette's birth, Grandmother had dreamed of Suzette paddling a canoe across stormy waters.

Suzette swallowed a sigh. "*Eya,* Grandmother? Yes?"

"When I was your age, I was more interested in helping my mother than following my father."

Suzette opened her mouth, closed it again, and finally answered, "*Eya,* Grandmother." Suzette didn't always think the same way Grandmother did, but she respected her, so she tried hard not to disagree with her out loud.

"Suzette worries about helping both of her parents," Mama said, before Grandmother could offer any more objections. "Don't worry, Suzette. Papa will be—"

As if in answer, Suzette heard a shout, and Papa burst from the trees. "*Mes amis!* My friends!" he bellowed. "They are coming!"

Suzette scrambled to her feet. The *voyageurs*! "Did you see them, Papa?"

"No." He was breathless. "I heard them singing. Faint. Just a whisper. But I heard it, across the water. They're coming!" He squinted at the fading sun. "Not today. Tomorrow." He grabbed his wife's hands and began to dance a jig.

Suzette laughed. Papa's shouts drew some of their neighbors, and soon a circle of people were stamping their feet as Papa led Mama in the wild dance.

Suddenly Papa stopped. "I'll paddle out to meet them!" he exclaimed, his face like a little boy's at sugaring time. "Yellow Wing, will you come with me?"

"I fear we'll have no peace otherwise!" Yellow Wing laughed. "May we at least eat an evening meal first?"

"We'll eat in the canoe!" Papa yelled.

Everyone was laughing. Suzette felt a flush of pride. Was there any man more full of life than her papa?

While Papa fetched blankets, Mama filled a pouch with pemmican, a mixture of fat, pounded venison, and dried cranberries. Papa kissed his baby daughter, then Suzette, then his wife. Then he and Yellow Wing retrieved one of the canoes, tucked their paddles inside, and lifted it onto their shoulders. Suzette and Mama followed them to the water's edge and watched while they splashed into the shallows and stepped into the canoe.

"We'll be back tomorrow," Papa called as they began to paddle, "and I'll bring the *voyageurs* with me! You be ready for some singing and some dancing!"

"We will!" Suzette cried, waving with all her might. Singing, dancing, feasting—and most important of all, the end of the trappers' competition! She could hardly wait.

By the next high sun, everyone knew the *voyageurs* were close. The island seemed to ripple with excitement. Suzette carried a sitting mat outside and tried to fill the time by working on a vest she was making for Papa. She had cleaned and tanned and sewn the soft deerskin herself, and was carefully stitching tiny glass beads in a colorful band around the bottom.

"A'jawac," Grandmother said. "You should practice

your quillwork." She was roasting a speared trout, and she eyed Suzette over the flames of the cook fire. "Those beads are not as attractive." Grandmother made designs the old way, using dyed porcupine quills instead of the beads the Ojibwe women got from the trading post.

"I could never do such lovely quillwork as you, Grandmother," Suzette said, poking among the shells where she had sorted her beads by color. "But I wish I had purple beads. These blue ones aren't right for the design."

"The traders don't have purple beads," Mama pointed out calmly. She lifted Charlotte from her cradleboard.

"But I think I've seen someone with purple beading. On moccasins." Suzette cocked her head, trying to remember. "I can picture them. So *someone* has them. I just can't remember who they belong to." Beaded moccasins were worn only for special occasions. "I want the vest to be perfect! I'm going to give it to Papa when he wins the competition."

"*If* he wins the competition," Mama corrected. "There are many fine trappers."

"But, Mama, he *has* to win!" Suzette could hardly sit still, knowing the winner would soon be announced. She slipped the vest back into a storage bag. She couldn't bear to sit and *think,* not one moment longer! "Mama, I want to go to the beach to wait for the *voyageurs.* May I, please?" She was away almost before Mama nodded.

Many people were heading to the beach in front of the fort. As Suzette neared the stockade, she heard someone call her name. "*Bonjour,* Suzette!" It was a French man named Big Nicolas. His name was a joke, since he was even shorter than most *voyageurs.* He was sitting on a rock near the beach as if deep in thought, smoking his pipe.

"*Bonjour,* Big Nicolas!" Suzette wondered, not for the first time, if he was sad. Big Nicolas had broken his arm in a bad fall the summer before and couldn't paddle back to Montréal, so the fur-trade company had discharged him. He had spent a surely lonely winter trapping on the mainland. Suzette didn't know Big Nicolas well, but she had never heard him complain. He was the kind of man who found time to carve dolls for little girls or pull a woman's sled if he thought her load was too heavy.

With a wave, Suzette hurried on to the landing. A crowd was gathering at the beach where the *voyageurs* would arrive. Old women were mending fishnets, and young women were tending babies. Children splashed in and out of the water. Older boys paddled canoes wildly near the landing, showing off. And clustered near the water's edge were the people waiting most eagerly—several women who had married *voyageurs,* and their children.

Suzette spotted her friend among them. "Gabrielle!" She hurried over.

"Listen!" Gabrielle said.

Suzette shivered with excitement as she heard a snatch of song. She knew she wouldn't be able to see the *voyageurs* until they rounded the long point of land that sheltered the beach from the rough open water of the great lake. But she could *hear* them.

Gabrielle grabbed her hand. "Oh, Suzette, it's so hard to wait. If only I knew that my papa—"

"I see them!" one of the boys cried.

Yes! Suzette squinted into the sunlight glinting off the water and slowly counted eight sixteen-man canoes as they rounded the point from the east and headed toward the beach. The *voyageurs* were bellowing a favorite French song. Papa and Yellow Wing darted among them in their smaller, lighter canoe. Suzette could see Papa singing with his friends, and she raised her voice in a whoop. How wonderful to see Papa so happy again!

The *voyageurs* drew closer, and women began to wave as they caught sight of their husbands. "Papa!" Gabrielle squealed, and Suzette grinned. On command, the *voyageurs* lifted their paddles and raised their voices in a unison yell of joy. Then they were paddling again, with short, hard strokes.

Soldiers and laborers from the post joined the Ojibwe and *Métis* people already on the beach. The carpenter was fiercely scratching out a tune on his fiddle. Three Ojibwe men were beating hand drums and singing. A group of *Métis* women and children in doeskin leggings and cotton dresses of scarlet and blue were dancing. Two of the young fort laborers began to jig.

Suzette watched Captain d'Amboise parade solemnly to the landing, wearing a fine blue-and-white uniform instead of his usual leathers. He was a big man whose position demanded respect, and whose abilities earned it.

D'Amboise was accompanied by Baptiste, a *Métis* man who was the fort interpreter. Although d'Amboise was learning Ojibwe, he relied on Baptiste for important occasions. Baptiste spoke not only Ojibwe and French, but Fox, Sioux, Huron, and Menominee as well. Unlike d'Amboise, Baptiste was dressed as usual: leather moccasins and leggings, beaded knee bands, a colorful calico shirt, and a red headband tied around his forehead.

The huge canoes drew close to the landing. Young Ojibwe men ran to help as some of the *voyageurs* jumped into the shallow water to lug the bundles and barrels— filled with supplies and trade goods—to shore. The instant their duties were tended, *voyageurs* with families waiting joyfully embraced their wives and children.

Suzette ran to Papa and Yellow Wing as they beached their canoe. "You found your friends, Papa!"

"*Oui!*" Papa grinned. "*Mon Dieu,* it's good to be among them again! Tonight we'll celebrate, eh?"

"And when the competition ends, we'll have even more to celebrate!" Suzette exclaimed. Papa put a finger over his lips and winked, then cocked his head toward Captain d'Amboise, who was about to speak.

D'Amboise smiled broadly, giving everyone a few moments to settle down. Then he raised his voice for the formal greeting. "*Bonjour! Aaniin!* On behalf of everyone at

Fort La Pointe, on behalf of our Ojibwe friends, I welcome you all!" Baptiste repeated the greeting in Ojibwe.

Everyone cheered, and d'Amboise raised his hand for quiet once again. "And let me remind all the trappers that the competition will be closed tomorrow at high sun. Anyone who still has furs to turn in for credit must report to Monsieur Roussain by that time. He will tally the ledgers, and whoever has the highest count wins! The winner will be announced tomorrow night!"

Suzette squeezed Papa's hand. He winked again.

"Now," Captain d'Amboise concluded, "I want all these bundles and kegs carried safely into the fort. Once they're stowed, I am releasing everyone from their duties for the rest of the day!" The *voyageurs* whooped before starting to load the heavy cargo into waiting handcarts.

Then Suzette noticed Monsieur Roussain hurrying from the fort. Unlike everyone else on the beach, he was not smiling. His grim expression made her uneasy.

Roussain stopped by Captain d'Amboise and leaned close, whispering. The smile faded from d'Amboise's face. He shook his head. Then he snapped his fingers at one of the nearby soldiers and said something Suzette couldn't hear. The soldier fired his gun into the air, and the crowd suddenly hushed.

"I'm sorry to disturb your fun," Captain d'Amboise said grimly, "but I have an announcement to make. A sorry announcement." Even the muted chatter died away.

Suzette saw surprise, concern, and confusion on her friends' faces as Baptiste interpreted. She felt as if a shadow had crossed the sun.

"I'm very sad to say that a theft has occurred," Captain d'Amboise went on. "Monsieur Roussain has just discovered that some furs have been stolen from the storage room." A shocked murmur rose from the crowd.

"I will begin an investigation immediately." D'Amboise's voice was hard as iron. "When the thief is discovered, he will be punished severely. I will send paddlers to the camps and distant forts to tell the story. He will be welcome nowhere." The people on the beach nodded approvingly. Suzette caught her breath. Banishment—being cut off from family, clan, tribe—was too terrible to think about.

"One more thing. Because of the theft, I am forced to announce that the trappers' competition must be canceled."

Suzette felt the captain's words like a blow. *No!*

Protests rose up from the crowd. Captain d'Amboise shook his head. "I'm sorry. But there's no way to be sure that any furs turned in tomorrow don't include stolen furs. I have no choice."

With that he turned and walked into the fort. Baptiste and Monsieur Roussain followed. After a moment of stunned silence, the crowd began to break up—the *voyageurs* finishing with the goods and canoes, families drifting away. Gabrielle walked by, clinging to her father.

Finally, it seemed that only Suzette and her father

were standing still. "Oh, Papa!" she breathed. "What are we going to do?" The competition probably didn't matter so much to anyone else. No doubt many trappers hadn't even paid attention to it. Those who had were excited by the challenge. But surely no one else had all their hopes for the future riding on that contest!

Papa's broad shoulders sagged in a way they never had before, even when carrying the heaviest load. "It seems there is nothing to do," he whispered. "Without that prize, I have no way to pay my debt to the company. At the end of the summer, I'll be paddling back to Montréal."

"Papa, *non!*"

He rubbed his eyes. "I'm sorry, Suzette," he managed, and kissed the top of her head. "I must go find your mama now. Don't worry. Everything will be well in the end."

He walked away like an old man.

That evening, the festivities of *rendez-vous* began, but Suzette's family stayed at their campsite, sitting silently around a low fire. The Ojibwe campground was empty. The *voyageurs'* shouts and songs drifted from the grounds in front of the fort. She could picture the bonfires on the beach, the women preparing a feast.

"It will be all right," Mama said finally. "We have managed every winter before now."

"Of course it will be all right," Papa echoed, but his voice was hollow as a reed whistle. From across the meadow, Suzette could hear snatches of laughter and song. Usually Papa was in the middle of the celebration, for he was the loudest singer, the best storyteller, the liveliest dancer. It hurt Suzette's heart to see him sitting cross-legged with his head in his hands.

"Maybe Captain d'Amboise will find the stolen furs," Yellow Wing suggested.

"Yes. Maybe." Papa didn't sound hopeful.

Grandmother stroked Suzette's hair. Mama poured some tea. As they stared at the flames, an extra-loud burst of laughter drifted through the trees.

Suzette clenched her fists on her knees. "Maybe there's something we can do to help him find the furs," she said finally.

"There is nothing to do," Papa sighed. "Captain d'Amboise made the right decision. The only fair decision."

"It's not fair to us!"

"A'jawac," Grandmother murmured, frowning.

"Sometimes we must learn to accept things," Mama added. "Do not fight clouds, daughter."

Suzette knew she should listen in silence to her elders and honor them by trying to accept this, as they wished. But she just couldn't bear to sit by the fire and accept defeat.

CHAPTER 5
UNDER SUSPICION

After a morning meal of flatbread, Suzette walked through the Ojibwe camp to the post for a French lesson.

Outside the fort, some *voyageurs* were snoring beneath their overturned canoes or little canvas shelters, sleeping off their night of celebrating. Several soldiers trudged past, hauling loads of firewood from the forest. By the fort gate, Suzette stepped aside to make way for two Ojibwe men carrying a dead doe slung on a pole. The hunters had been hired by Captain d'Amboise to provide food for the French. As she waited for them to enter, she saw an Ojibwe woman who cooked for the soldiers heading out toward the garden, carrying a hoe. Children darted back and forth in some sort of game. A family who had evidently already visited the store that morning walked back toward camp, carrying a new kettle and a length of calico.

Suzette stared at the commotion as if seeing it for the first time. No one looked at her as she entered the stockade. How easy it could be for a thief to slip into the fort unnoticed! But who would have stolen the furs?

With a sigh, she walked on to the store and found Monsieur Roussain talking to his friend Baptiste, the interpreter. "*Bonjour, bonjour,*" she said.

"Ah, Suzette, you do not belong here in the wilderness," Roussain sighed, leaning on the counter. He was so tall and thin he gave the impression of folding. "You should be walking the streets of Paris, *non?* With a parasol, and perhaps a lady's maid in tow. Living in a fine house."

Suzette shook her head. She had no wish to live in a fine French house.

"You should listen to Roussain," Baptiste told her. "La Pointe is not a place to spend your whole life."

"Perhaps," Suzette said politely. Baptiste had little patience for children. She didn't bother to tell him there was no place she liked better than La Pointe!

Baptiste turned back to Roussain. "I just stopped by to get some provisions. Captain d'Amboise asked me to head out to see what I can find out about the theft."

Suzette felt a flicker of hope. "Where are you going?" she asked eagerly, then bit her lip. It wasn't polite for a girl to question an adult.

He shrugged. "To visit some of the trappers. Ask some questions. I know many people. I may discover something."

Suzette waited while Monsieur Roussain gave his friend a twist of tobacco and a packet of dried venison. "Good luck," Suzette called as the interpreter left. He waved his hand.

"Don't despair yet, Suzette," Roussain said sympathetically. "If anyone can learn something about the theft, it's Baptiste. He knows everyone. Now, there's much to do this morning. Let's forget about trouble and get to work, eh?"

Suzette managed a smile. She could tell that Monsieur Roussain knew what was on her mind. It felt good to have such a friend.

"I need to inventory all the new goods the *voyageurs* brought," the clerk said. "You can help me."

He opened one of his big ledgers on the counter and showed her the right page. Then he pried the lid from a barrel and began unpacking the goods inside. Suzette dipped a pen into the little bottle of ink and carefully wrote each new item in the inventory column as Roussain laid them on the counter: needles, kettles, silver jewelry, blankets, gunpowder, traps, flints and fire steels, tobacco, candles, guns. But she couldn't forget about the canceled competition—not when everyone who walked into the store wanted to talk with Roussain about the theft.

"That is a very bad business, *non?*" asked a *voyageur* who came in for pipe tobacco. "How many furs were stolen?"

Suzette paused from counting new wool blankets to hear the clerk's answer. "A bale," Roussain told him. Suzette was startled. A whole bale? Bales weighed as much as she did! They might include a bear skin and several dozen smaller pelts, or as many as sixty beaver skins.

"Who could have done such a thing?" wondered the post blacksmith, who had stopped by to see if the *voyageurs* had brought the new hammer he'd requested last autumn.

"It must have been one of the trappers," the *voyageur* said. "Someone who wants very much to win that prize."

Suzette sighed. Dozens of trappers brought their furs to Fort La Pointe.

When the morning's inventory was complete, Suzette helped Roussain arrange the new goods on the shelves lining every wall. They were interrupted when Niskigwun carried an armload of furs into the store. Suzette felt her face grow hot. She hadn't seen Niskigwun since she'd bumped his canoe with her basket.

"*Aaniin*," Monsieur Roussain said in greeting. He didn't speak Ojibwe well, but he always greeted his customers in their own language. They liked him for it. "What do you have for me today?"

Niskigwun put his furs on the counter. "Three beaver, one mink, one otter. But I'm unhappy that they won't count toward the competition. I think I would have won."

Suzette bit her tongue. *What a braggart!* she thought. *Papa would have been the winner!*

"You may write Niskigwun's furs in the ledger," Roussain told her.

Suzette turned the pages until she found the sheet where Niskigwun's pelts were recorded. Stewing inside, she dutifully wrote down his furs. But while Niskigwun and Monsieur Roussain discussed the value of the pelts, Suzette silently scanned Niskigwun's page in the ledger and counted the number of pelts he had already been credited with. Had he really done well enough to win the prize?

Of all the animals trapped for their fur, beaver were the most desirable. Most trappers brought in perhaps fifty beaver pelts in a year. Suzette's father had managed to accumulate almost twice that number. Niskigwun hadn't done quite as well. But he was close.

Close enough that one bale of stolen furs might have made the difference!

Suzette's skin tingled as she realized what the ledger in her hands could tell her. The man who had stolen the bale of furs had probably been trying to win the contest. If she looked through the ledger and saw which trappers were close, and which were so far behind that even a bale of stolen furs wouldn't have helped, she might narrow the list of possible thieves.

It wasn't much to go on. But it was a start.

"You went through the ledger?" Gabrielle asked.

Suzette had been so excited about her discovery that she'd rushed to find her friend, needing to talk. The two girls were sitting in the sun near Gabrielle's lodge. Gabrielle's mother had asked them to tend a low, smoky fire under a rack where pieces of fish were drying. "Did Monsieur Roussain know what you were doing?"

"Not exactly," Suzette admitted. "But I always help him with the ledgers. There's nothing secret about it."

"Did you learn anything?"

"Maybe." Suzette looked over her shoulder to make sure no one could overhear. "It looked like just a handful of trappers were really trying to win that prize. Only two were very close to Papa's numbers, though. Niskigwun and Big Nicolas."

"You think that one of them is the thief?" Gabrielle's eyes were wide. "But why? Why would either one do such a thing?"

Suzette thought for a moment. Gabrielle was right. Who would do such a terrible thing just to win a prize? "Well . . . that Niskigwun might have wanted to win just so he could brag about how good a trapper he is."

"What about—*ugh!*" The breeze had suddenly shifted, blowing smoke into the girls' faces, and they scrambled to the other side of the fire. "What about Big Nicolas?"

Suzette rubbed her forehead. "Maybe he had a special reason to want the prize, like Papa did. Maybe—maybe he needed the prize to pay his passage back to Montréal, since he can't work as a *voyageur* anymore."

Gabrielle nodded. "That could be. So what are you going to do now?"

"I've been trying to figure that out." Suzette flexed her fingers, thinking out loud. "The thief probably planned to claim the furs as his own and bring them in to Monsieur Roussain just before the competition ended. Now that it's been canceled, what happens to the furs?"

Gabrielle waved an arm at several hopeful seagulls. "The thief turns them in anyway? At least he'd get regular credit for them at the store."

Suzette thought that over. "Of course the thief wouldn't bring in the whole bale at once, or everyone would know they were the stolen furs. He must be hiding the furs somewhere, so he can turn in just a few at a time." She chewed her lip. Niskigwun had brought furs to the store that very morning! "Gabrielle, I've got to find the hiding place before the thief turns in all the furs—"

"But even if you found furs, how would you know they were the stolen ones?" Gabrielle asked. "Many of the trappers may have held some furs back, wanting to turn them in at the last moment."

Suzette nodded. Her own papa had done so. "Then I need to find out more about that bale of furs."

"How are you going to do that?"

"I don't know. But, Gabrielle, I've *got* to! If I don't,

Papa will have to leave at the end of trading season!" When Suzette saw the look on her friend's face, she wished she could snatch the words back. Gabrielle's papa was going to leave, just as he did every year. "Oh, Gabrielle, I'm sorry."

"I know. I understand how important it is for you." Gabrielle stared at the fire.

Suzette sighed, knowing she'd been thoughtless. "I'd better go. Mama might need my help."

Almost everyone she passed on the walk back to her own lodge smiled or called a greeting, but Suzette answered absently. Her mind was filled with the picture of herself standing beside Gabrielle on the beach, waving good-bye as the *voyageurs* paddled away to Montréal. She didn't even notice the French soldier standing beside her lodge until she was almost upon it. Her sadness turned to unease.

Something was wrong.

She ran the rest of the way and found her mother and grandmother standing by the entrance to the *wiigwam,* near the soldier. A few Ojibwe people were ringed behind them. "What's wrong?" Suzette whispered anxiously.

"Be silent." Mama was holding Charlotte but freed a hand to place on Suzette's shoulder.

Suzette heard a mutter of men's voices from inside. Then the blanket over the opening was pushed aside. Captain d'Amboise emerged, followed by her father and Yellow Wing.

"You see, you found nothing in either of our lodges,"

Yellow Wing said angrily. "You're making false accusations."
Yellow Wing didn't speak much French, and Captain
d'Amboise didn't speak much Ojibwe, so Papa translated.
Worry gnawed Suzette's stomach as she listened to the
same words in two languages. False accusations about what?

Grandmother stepped forward and faced Captain
d'Amboise. "My son Yellow Wing is not a thief," she said.
"Neither is my French son. You bring dishonor. You dishonor yourself by accusing two good men. These men
work hard. They are respected."

Grandmother spoke slowly. Captain d'Amboise looked
as if he wanted to interrupt, but he listened quietly during
the speech and translation. At least he knew to respect
elders. Some French men weren't so wise.

But he didn't back down. "I must investigate this theft,"
d'Amboise said finally. "It seems the furs were stolen some-
time during the night before last. Almost every other man
on this island was seen that night by dozens of people." He
looked from Papa to Yellow Wing. "Everyone but you two."

"I told you, we went to meet the *voyageurs*! Ask any
of them!" Papa spat out the words.

"I will. However, they are your friends. And for you
two to slip back around the island before you met them,
wait for a quiet moment . . . it is not impossible." He
sighed. "I'm sorry, Philippe. But I know how desperate
you were to win that prize. And now, the first theft we've
ever had . . . and during a time when no one but your

brother-in-law can truly account for your whereabouts . . .
it doesn't look good."

Papa's face had grown red as a loon's eye while Captain
d'Amboise spoke. "Are you charging me with this crime?"

"*Non.* I can prove nothing. I'm asking questions,
nothing more."

"Then leave my lodge!" Papa shouted. Suzette felt
Mama's fingers squeezing her shoulder. Charlotte began
to cry. Mama was probably squeezing her too.

Captain d'Amboise nodded soberly, beckoned to the
soldier, and walked away.

Suzette couldn't bear it any longer. "Oh, Papa!" she
cried, and ran to his side. "How can they think—"

"Suzette," Mama murmured. "Let your papa be."

Papa smoothed her black hair away from her forehead.
"Don't worry, Suzette. I—I just . . ." He looked at the
circle of anxious faces. "I need to be alone." He walked
quickly away, disappearing into the trees.

Suzette watched him go, feeling miserable. D'Amboise's
hard words at the landing pounded through her head.
*When the thief is discovered, he will be punished severely. I will
send paddlers to the camps and distant forts to tell the story. He
will be welcome nowhere.*

Chapter 6
A Surprising Discovery

Suzette couldn't sleep until she heard Papa creep inside the *wiigwam* late that night. When she woke at first light the next morning, he was gone again.

The rest of the family was already outside. Mama was frying flatbread for the morning meal. "Where's Papa?" Suzette asked her.

"On the lake. It is the best place for him right now." Mama's voice was understanding, but sad.

"He should have taken me with him," Yellow Wing muttered. "If he's guilty, I'm guilty too."

"No one in this family is guilty!" Mama pinched her lips in a tight line and slapped a ball of dough on her rolling stone so hard that the dough crumbled. Suzette stared at the ground. Mama never spoke in such a tone! Suzette felt as if her family was crumbling just like the dough.

Suzette knew her father had not stolen the furs. But d'Amboise believed he could have! If the true thief was

not found, her father might be banished. Where would
he take his family? Deeper into the woods on the mainland, away from his beloved lake, away from their own
band of Ojibwe people? Could they survive? Would they
be welcome anywhere?

Suddenly Two Fish's forgotten insult rang in her mind.
*Blue Eyes! You are an ugly girl. I'm glad you're not my sister. I'd
be ashamed.* She had shrugged his words aside at the time,
but now they sliced into her heart. What if other people
felt the way Two Fish felt?

She clenched her fists. Away from La Pointe, would
her blue eyes always mark her as different? She couldn't
hide who she was, but she suddenly wished she could.
If only Papa were Ojibwe too—

No! Suzette felt her face burn with shame. She might
wish she had beautiful dark eyes like Mama's, but she
could *never* wish her father was anyone but Papa—

"Suzette!" Mama was staring at her. "Are you listening?
I want you to finish the flatbread. And I need you to tend
Charlotte this morning. Grandmother and I promised to
help some of the other women in the garden."

"*Eya,* Mama," Suzette sighed. It was her responsibility
to help with Charlotte, and she hadn't done much of
that lately.

Yellow Wing stayed behind too. After eating, he
brought out a fish trap that needed repairing. Suzette
settled Charlotte on a blanket in the shade. Cleaning up

from the morning meal didn't take long, and she didn't have the heart to work on Papa's beaded vest.

Finally she settled down in the shade with a red shirt of Papa's that needed mending. Slipping the needle in and out of the fabric occupied her hands and left her mind free to wrestle with the family's problems. Too much had happened since they'd left the mainland—first the canoe that almost capsized, then the theft that robbed Papa of his chance to pay off his debt.

Yellow Wing muttered and swatted away a mosquito. Suzette let her sewing rest, regarding him. He would know the other men on the island better than anyone else she could ask. "Yellow Wing . . . may I ask you a question?"

"Just don't ask me about the furs." He shifted the fish trap on his lap and tried to weave a branch into place. It snapped, and he tossed it into the fire.

"Do you know Niskigwun well?"

"No. Why?"

"He's not very nice."

Yellow Wing's mouth twitched toward a smile. "Maybe he just doesn't like disrespectful girls."

Suzette made a face. She knew she sometimes talked more than was proper, but she was never as rude as Niskigwun—or his son! "Yesterday at the trading post he was bragging that he would have won the contest if it hadn't been canceled."

"Niskigwun can be full of his own glories," Yellow Wing

agreed. "But he's also a very skillful trapper. He probably had a good chance."

Suzette swallowed her disappointment. She had wanted Yellow Wing to tell her that Niskigwun was desperate to win—that he had wagered his canoe on the competition, or something like that. She had been foolish to even think it might be so simple! With a heavy sigh, Suzette picked up her sewing again.

Yellow Wing must have heard her. "Suzette, I don't know if your papa trapped more furs than Niskigwun over the winter," he said gently. "But I do know that your papa is an honest man who works hard for his family. He did as well as any man in his place could have."

"I know." Suzette forced herself to study her sewing, taking the tiny stitches Mama had taught her, and tried again to figure out how to bend the conversation where she wanted it to go. "But he doesn't like trapping. It's been hard for him. I think it's difficult for any *voyageur* who has to give up paddling. Like Big Nicolas. He knows his arm will never be strong enough for him to be a *voyageur* again."

"I've never heard him complain." Yellow Wing picked up the trap again.

"I imagine he'd like to go back to Montréal, if he could," Suzette suggested.

But Yellow Wing shook his head. "No. Just the opposite. Shortly after we crossed from the mainland, he was asking a number of us lots of questions about the island. What the country was like. Whether there was any open land. Whether there were any caves. How long it took to walk across it. How much copper was in the soil. He was taking a strong interest in the island for someone dreaming of leaving it."

"Oh." So Big Nicolas was not desperately trying to win the prize so he could buy passage back to Montréal. Suzette sat back on her heels, disappointed again. Nothing made sense.

By the time Mama and Grandmother returned, Suzette had tidied the lodge and fixed a kettle of dried Juneberries simmered with maple sugar. "Mama, may I go to the trading post?" she asked. She didn't know *where* to look for the stolen furs, but she could still try to find out exactly *what* she was looking for. The only person who could help her with that was Monsieur Roussain.

As Suzette was leaving, Grandmother shook her head at Mama. "Shining Stone, it would be better if you didn't let A'jawac spend so much time learning the French language. I worry that she is walking down the wrong path."

"I've tried to teach her well," Mama said quietly. "And she has learned many things from you. But Suzette is *Métis*. Both Ojibwe and French. Her papa has different ideas . . ."

Suzette pretended she hadn't heard, and hurried away.

She wanted to respect Grandmother's feelings, but she didn't understand why Grandmother was so often critical of French ways. Hadn't she chosen a French man for her first husband? Besides, Suzette enjoyed her time spent with Monsieur Roussain—and now, her lessons had taken on new importance. Perhaps those ledgers held the answers she was looking for.

She arrived at the store as Monsieur Roussain was showing several families some of the new trade goods. She hesitated in the doorway, suddenly uncertain. Her teacher had surely heard that Captain d'Amboise had searched their camp the evening before. Perhaps—

"Suzette!" Roussain called. "I'm glad you're here. I could use your help."

Relieved, Suzette joined him behind the counter. At his direction, she carefully wrote each customer's transactions in the ledger.

"You're doing well," Roussain said, looking over her entries after all the customers had left.

"*Merci, monsieur.*" His praise made her feel good. "I like reading and writing."

He rubbed his chin with ink-stained fingers. "I should loan you a book. One with stories in it. Would you like that? Stories would help pass the time, especially in winter. You must get terribly bored."

"Bored?" Suzette hesitated. "I'm sure I would enjoy a book with stories in it, *monsieur.* It's kind of you to think of it. But we *do* have stories! Grandmother is a wonderful storyteller, and Yellow Wing . . .”

Her voice trailed away as another Ojibwe family came in. She watched Roussain show them the newly arrived bolts of cloth. Did he understand? Yes, winters could be bitterly cold and quiet in the little family camp deep in the woods. But winter was also a time to snuggle around the fire in their warm *wiigwam* and listen to the elders tell wonderful tales of how things came to be. Did he think Ojibwe people had no stories just because they weren’t written down with letters?

I’ll explain it to him one day, Suzette thought. But she could see it needed to wait until another time, when he wasn’t so busy—and she didn’t already have so much on her mind.

“I’m glad you came by,” Monsieur Roussain said when they were alone again. “I’ve been busy since sunup. In addition to everyone wanting to see the new goods the *voyageurs* brought, all the trappers have been bringing in their last loads of furs. I’m trying to get the pelts baled up and inventoried back in the storage room, and—”

“I can help you with that,” Suzette offered. Maybe she could find a record of the stolen furs!

“Good.” He pushed open the door behind the counter and led her into the storage room.

“Oh!” Suzette exclaimed. “I’ve never seen it so full!” Many trappers must have come by in the past day or so, for the narrow room was almost bursting with pelts: beaver, bear, deer, muskrat, otter, raccoon. Some were hanging from poles suspended from the ceiling. Some were stacked on the floor.

"As I said, we're behind." Roussain sighed, pointing to two sweaty laborers working at the huge fur press that squatted in the middle of the floor. "They're pressing furs into bales. Michel! Make sure that bale is pressed tight! There's no spare room in the canoes."

Suzette watched as the men finished pressing the furs and tied thin rope securely around the stack. One of the laborers hauled the bale over to the wall near Roussain's high desk. The other man carefully placed a piece of paper on top of the bale, tucking a corner beneath the rope binding.

As the men began gathering furs to press into the next bale, she went to look at the row of finished, hip-tall bales near the desk. She tried to lift one. Too heavy! Each of these bales had a piece of paper lying on it, and she slid one free to examine: *1 bear, 12 deer, 32 beaver, 3 otter.*

"We make an inventory list of the furs packed into each bale," Roussain explained as he joined her. He opened a big ledger on his desk. "Each of those inventories needs to be copied into this ledger. Then the original list gets tucked under the rope, and the bale is wrapped securely with burlap and tied again." He pointed to the far wall, where a huge pile of neatly packaged bales were already awaiting the *voyageurs'* departure. "Clerks in Montréal check the contents again when the furs are unpacked." Roussain thumbed through the ledger. "Here. This is where I left off."

Suzette looked at the ledger page, covered with Roussain's neat writing. "*Monsieur?*" she asked. "Is there a record of the stolen furs?"

"I'm afraid not. I knew when one bale was missing because I knew how many we had. I had made an inventory list, but I hadn't had time to copy it into the ledger."

"Oh." Suzette felt flooded with disappointment. How could anyone track the stolen furs if they didn't even know what to look for?

Roussain sat on a bale. "My little friend, try not to worry."

Suzette struggled to contain her frustration. "I'm afraid we'll never find the answer, and then . . ." Her voice trailed away. "Did you know that Captain d'Amboise suspects Papa?"

Roussain seemed to pick his words carefully. "I know he asked questions." He studied the floor for a moment, then sighed. "Suzette, keeping busy may be the best thing for you right now. Work on copying these inventory lists into the ledger, eh? Mark an X on each as you finish, so I'll know which have been entered. And maybe I'll make some *chocolat*. You'd like that, *non?*"

Suzette tried to smile. She didn't want to hurt her friend's feelings. He considered it a great treat to serve the warm *chocolat* drink. It would take more than that, however, to make her forget the theft. "But *monsieur,* you said you made an inventory list for the stolen bale. So it was still on top of the bale when it was stolen?"

Roussain rubbed his chin. "*Oui,* I suppose so. But—" Suddenly he turned his head; someone else had come into the next room. "I can't leave the store unattended. You stay here and begin working. Just don't get in the men's way."

Suzette nodded. Perched on the high stool at the desk, she began copying the first inventory list into the ledger. She worked carefully, trying not to make any blots. But thoughts of the missing inventory kept nudging into her mind. *Concentrate!* she scolded herself. Captain d'Amboise and Baptiste had been investigating the theft. If the thief hadn't noticed the inventory or known what it was, and it slipped onto the floor, they would have found it.

She began writing again, but when she misspelled the French word for otter—*loutre*—she put the pen aside for good. There was no harm in looking herself. She glanced quickly at the laborers. They were leaning on the handle of the fur press, grunting with exertion. Neither was paying any attention to her.

Suzette scrambled onto the nearest bale and stretched her arm into the crevice between it and the wall. She searched along the whole row of bales, cramming her fingers into cracks, peering into dim corners. Then she searched along the route from the bales to the door, looking under work tables and behind piles of furs.

Nothing.

She sat back on her stool, trying to think. One of the laborers lit his pipe, snatching a break during Roussain's absence. Squeals from some children's ball game drifted through the window at the back of the room—

The window! Suzette jumped to her feet. The post's only glass windows were in Captain d'Amboise's room and in the store. The storage room window had wooden shutters only, barred from the inside. Maybe the thief hadn't calmly carried the bale out the front door, which led into the open common area of the fort. Maybe he'd climbed out the window.

When the laborers went back to work, Suzette walked the length of the room toward the window. No sign of the lost inventory. She chewed her lip, considering. If the thief had grabbed a bale in the dark and lugged it to the window . . . he probably dropped it out the window, then climbed out himself. She checked the floor near the low window, then leaned over the sill, scanning the narrow length of dirt between the storage room and the stockade wall. Nothing.

And then she saw it. Not on the open ground, but beneath a honeysuckle bush growing against the wall near the window. At least it *might* be the lost inventory—all she could see was a corner of dirty white paper.

She leaned out the open window, stretching. Almost got it . . . not quite . . . "Ooof!" she grunted as the window-sill cut into her belly. She almost lost her balance, and for one wild moment she thought she was going to tumble out into the yard. Then she pinched the slip of paper and slid back into the room.

The two laborers were staring at her.

"I was just—just looking for something," Suzette said, feeling her face flush. They rolled their eyes at each other and went back to work. Suzette turned away and quickly examined the paper. It was crumpled and dirty, with one corner missing. But it was an inventory!

She scanned the French words. *One black bear, 40 beaver—* "Oh!" she gasped. The inventory contained an odd note. *Three of these beaver have a noticeable golden streak down the back. Almost a stripe. Very unusual. Two credits each.*

Suzette wanted to dance. Now she knew what to search for! She started to run triumphantly into the other room to show Roussain. The babble of voices stopped her. She didn't want everyone on the island talking about this discovery.

For some reason, her grandmother's words about wasting her time learning to read French popped into her mind. "You're wrong, Grandmother," she whispered triumphantly. If she could find the beaver pelts with golden stripes, she would find the thief.

CHAPTER 7

A DANGEROUS PLAN

Suzette was about to walk back into the store when she recognized Captain d'Amboise's voice. "Any more trouble?"

"No, sir," Roussain said. Suzette stopped near the door, just out of sight. She didn't want to talk to d'Amboise.

"I hear that Jacques Dupré has set up a camp on the northeast end of the island, beyond Big Bay. I don't like the sound of that. I'm going to send Baptiste and one of the soldiers to pay a visit. Dupré has no business here. When an illegal trader sets up camp so close to Fort La Pointe, it means trouble."

"I don't think he can really compete with us here at the post," Roussain pointed out. "The Indian people know they get fair trade for their pelts here, and quality goods in return. They have no reason to start going elsewhere."

"Well, keep an eye on the books," Captain d'Amboise said firmly. "If people suddenly stop trading here, I want to know about it. We'll run that scoundrel off the island."

Suzette waited until she was sure d'Amboise was gone before she walked back into the store. "*Monsieur, look!*" She smoothed the paper out on the counter and told him how she'd found it. "I think it's the inventory from the stolen bale!"

"*Mon Dieu!*" he exclaimed. "I think you're right." He paused, reading the list. "Of course! I remember that batch! Those beaver pelts were very unusual. Someone brought them in from the mainland. Said they came from somewhere west of here. Baptiste said he'd never seen anything like them either. I didn't realize *those* were in the stolen bale."

Baptiste walked through the doorway. "What's this about the stolen bale?"

"Suzette found the inventory," Roussain told him. "Now we know exactly what furs were taken. Remember those pelts with the golden stripes?"

Baptiste looked startled. "Those were stolen?"

"Now we know what to look for," Suzette said eagerly. "Have you learned anything?" She held her breath, hoping the interpreter had good news.

But he shook his head. "I'm afraid not. I asked everyone. People sometimes trust me more than the regular fort men. I thought I might hear something." He spread his hands, shrugging. "But I didn't."

Discouragement weighed on her shoulders like a bear robe. Baptiste was smart and capable, a man everyone knew and trusted. If he couldn't learn anything, what chance did she have of finding the thief?

"I still find it hard to believe that anyone who trades at the fort would commit such a theft," Roussain said with a sigh.

Baptiste shrugged again. "I can think of several men who might have done it."

Was he thinking of Niskigwun and Big Nicolas? Or other people altogether? "If only—" Suzette began, then bit back the words.

Baptiste leaned against the counter and folded his arms. "You should stop wondering about it," he told her. "Give up. We'll probably never know who did it. It could have been almost any trapper on the island."

"*Non!*" Suzette cried. She wouldn't believe that!

"You're too young to understand," Baptiste said impatiently. "Times are changing. When I was a boy, men trapped furs so they could trade for what they needed. Cloth for a new shirt, or gunpowder, or a cooking kettle. But as the years went by, they got spoiled and greedy. Look at this!" He reached over the counter and picked up a handful of silver jewelry—earbobs, necklaces, bracelets. "This is what people want now. They are becoming more dependent on the French and their ways every year. I tell you, times are changing."

Roussain frowned at Baptiste, drumming his long fingers on the counter. "My friend, you sound sour. Don't take your frustrations out on the girl."

Baptiste slowly put down the jewelry. "Yes, you're right." He shook his head. "I grow weary of working for you French men. The trappers, who only come to the fort now and then, see only the good things the French men have brought. I see both sides. The good and the bad."

"Perhaps one day you'll move away from the French forts, on to the western country, as you've spoken of," Roussain said. "Leave us all behind, eh?"

"Ah, you would miss me then!" Baptiste grinned. "Roussain, I came for some of your good black tobacco. I gave all of mine away on this trip." Tobacco was often given as a gift of goodwill among Indian people.

After the interpreter had left the store, Roussain turned to Suzette. "Don't mind him," Roussain said gently. "He is frustrated."

"About the theft?" Suzette asked slowly. She was still mulling over the things Baptiste had said.

"In part. He hasn't found any answers. Captain d'Amboise isn't happy. Baptiste thinks Captain d'Amboise is harder on him than the other workers because he is *Métis*."

Métis like me, Suzette thought. Part French and part Ojibwe. Both and neither. "Do you think that's true?" she whispered. "About Captain d'Amboise?"

"I don't know. I'm not *Métis*. I find Captain d'Amboise a fair man to work for."

"Do you think Baptiste will really move on?" Suzette couldn't imagine him leaving. He knew everyone, knew where all the winter camps were.

Roussain smiled. "Oh, he dreams at times, as we all do. Baptiste dreams of heading west, setting out his own trap-lines, leaving the rest of us behind."

Was her friend and tutor thinking of leaving too? "What do you dream of, *monsieur?* Do you wish to move on as well?"

Roussain smiled. "Don't look so sad, Suzette. I'm here because I want to be. But perhaps sometimes I dream of traveling back to Montréal, or to Paris—as I have often suggested to you. I wish you could see what life is like there."

Suzette chewed her lip. Was this Montréal a place her family could go if Papa was banished? Papa said little of his former life there, or of his parents. But maybe . . . "Monsieur Roussain, what is it like in Montréal?"

"Well, it's a city. More people and buildings than you can imagine. Coaches and wagons and . . ." He spread his hands, as if at a loss for words.

"Do you think Mama would like it there? And Grandmother and Yellow Wing?"

"*Non,*" he said quietly. "*You* might come to like it, in time, since you have so much French blood. But I don't think they would be happy there. And I don't think they would be accepted."

"But why?" she demanded, overwhelmed with frustration. "The Ojibwe people accept Papa." Yellow Wing thought of Papa as a brother, and all of their family and friends had welcomed him. He had even been adopted into the Eagle Clan. But did some people, people like Two Fish, resent that too?

Monsieur Roussain opened his mouth, closed it again, and finally shrugged helplessly. "That's not a question I can answer, Suzette."

Just then an Ojibwe family came into the store. "I've promised my wife new silver for her ears," the man said proudly, pointing to the tray of earbobs. "You marked down the credit for my furs over the cold months. Now I will get the silver."

Suzette left as Roussain showed them the jewelry. *I wonder if Baptiste is right,* she thought, hearing the children exclaim in excitement as their mother tried on the new earbobs. Then Suzette shook her head. No, she wasn't ready to believe his ugly words. The Ojibwe trappers worked hard all winter. Maybe they did enjoy buying gifts for their family after the *voyageurs* arrived with new goods each spring. That didn't mean they were greedy—or capable of stealing furs!

Suzette kicked a rock angrily as she headed toward the fort gate. It was becoming clear that she couldn't count on Baptiste or Captain d'Amboise to find the thief. It sounded as if they had given up. Well, *she* wasn't giving up. And now she knew what kind of furs to look for.

But where should she look?

Suzette paused outside the fort, near the makeshift camp the *voyageurs* had pitched. She took a deep breath, considering, then approached a man leaning on one elbow, smoking his pipe. "*Pardonnez-moi.* Is Big Nicolas about?"

"Haven't seen him. Might be at his lodge." The man pointed.

Suzette hesitantly approached the *wiigwam* that Big Nicolas had built at the edge of the Ojibwe camp, near the *voyageurs'* shelters. "*Bonjour?*" she called. "Big Nicolas?" There was no answer, just the faint laughter of some men swapping stories nearby. The fire pit was cold. Did she dare search his lodge? Suzette felt her stomach twitch nervously as she squatted by the entrance.

Just a quick peek. There was no harm in that, was there? She pulled aside the deerskin hanging over the doorway and peered into the lodge. Although he had no woman to tend his things, it was tidy. Blankets were neatly folded, and several storage baskets lined the back wall. But other than a bear robe he obviously used for sleeping, she couldn't see any furs—

A heavy hand clamped on her shoulder. Suzette's heart jumped like a kernel of corn dropped in hot bear grease. She scrambled to her feet.

"What are you doing?" Big Nicolas was frowning.

"I was—that is—I was just . . ." She forced herself to take a deep breath. "I was looking for you." *Now think! Think of a reason why!*

Big Nicolas didn't look convinced. "What for?"

Suzette glanced over her shoulder as if to make sure no one could hear. "For Papa," she whispered. "I wanted to ask you to visit him. Try to cheer him up." Did he believe her? She hoped he couldn't hear her heart hammering. She had never been afraid of Big Nicolas before. Was she just feeling guilty for snooping? Or did he have something to hide?

The *voyageur*'s frown slowly turned into a glare. Suzette was just tensing to run when he turned his head toward the trading post. "I'm very angry at d'Amboise," he said finally. "No one believes Philippe is a thief."

As Big Nicolas promised to visit Papa, Suzette tried to hide her relief—and her disappointment that she hadn't found any answers.

There was one more place to look. She asked a passerby for directions to Niskigwun's lodge. Just before she reached it, though, she spotted him sitting by his cook fire, all alone. One look at his face, bent over a spear point he was shaping, stilled her feet. Even alone, intent on his task, Niskigwun looked angry. Try as she might, she couldn't think of any reason to start a conversation with him—no Ojibwe girl would approach a man and speak first—much less get a peek into his lodge. Feeling both relieved and defeated, she turned back toward home.

The Ojibwe camp in the big meadow was busy. Walking back to her lodge, Suzette passed women working together to scrape deer hides free of bits of blood and dirt. Some men shouted over a gambling game. A girl wandered among the lodges crying "*Memengwaa! Memengwaa!*" which meant "Butterfly! Butterfly!" Children were playing hide-and-seek, and the girl was asking the butterflies to help her find her playmates. *Maybe I should call upon* memengwaa *to help me find the furs,* Suzette thought. *I might have better luck.*

"Suzette!" the little girl called. "Will you play with us?"

"I can't," Suzette said, shaking her head regretfully. For a moment she wished she was still a carefree child too.

That afternoon Mama sent Suzette to the lakeshore with an armload of laundry and a kettle of strained ash-water. The weak lye solution would help clean the clothes. Suzette had just waded into the cold water when she heard Gabrielle calling her name. "Suzette!" Gabrielle ran to join her. "Your mother told me you were here. Some of the girls were hoping to play a game of double ball. I'll help you with your washing, and then maybe we can both play."

Usually Suzette loved to play this game, in which two sand-stuffed balls, connected by a leather thong, were tossed and caught on sticks the players carried. But she shook her head. "I don't think so. I'm still thinking about the stolen furs." She told Gabrielle about finding the inventory. "So now I know what to look for. Three beaver pelts with golden stripes. If I find them, I find the thief."

"Are you going to search the lodges of Niskigwun and Big Nicolas?"

"I tried!" Suzette exclaimed, and quickly explained what had happened.

Gabrielle shook her head. "It would be hard to hide those special beaver pelts so close to the trading post anyway."

"The furs must be hidden somewhere away from camp." Suzette paused from scrubbing Papa's red shirt. "But where?"

"They could be anywhere!" Gabrielle spread her hands helplessly. "A hollow tree, a thicket—anywhere! A man who knows the island could find many places to hide stolen furs."

"Niskigwun probably knows the island well. Big Nicolas wouldn't, since he hasn't spent as much time here, but—oh!" Suzette stared at her friend. "Yellow Wing told me that Big Nicolas was asking some of the men about the island. About the land, and whether there are any caves on the island. Gabrielle, what would make a better hiding spot for stolen furs? Do you know of any caves on the island?"

"No. But if there are any, my brother would know. The fort men hired him to hunt for them, so he's been all over the island."

"Will you ask him? It's a good place to begin. But . . ." Suzette's excitement faded again. "Those fur bales are so heavy! Big Nicolas couldn't have carried one. Not with his bad arm. Niskigwun could have—but he wasn't the one asking about the caves!"

"Maybe Big Nicolas had help," Gabrielle said, lifting a heavy wool blanket from Suzette's pile of laundry and sloshing it into the shallow water. "But, Suzette, maybe the furs are already gone. If the beaver pelts are so unusual, they must make the thief nervous. Maybe he threw them into the lake."

"Maybe," Suzette admitted. "But beaver pelts are valuable. I don't think a trapper would waste them. He may have hidden them, but he'd still want to get full trade value for them. He must know he can't bring them to the fort. Monsieur Roussain would recognize them. So what can he do with them?"

"Use them himself?"

"Not with those golden stripes. No, he'd need to trade them somewhere else." Suzette pounded Papa's red shirt against a rock, her thoughts pounding too. "The thief would have to find another trader." She dropped the shirt.

"Gabrielle! Just this morning, Captain d'Amboise said an illegal trader named Jacques Dupré had set up camp on the far side of the island! I'll bet the thief plans to trade the beaver pelts there! Gabrielle, that must be it!"

"An unlicensed trader?" Gabrielle shook her head as she tugged the blanket out of the water and spread it on a large, flat rock to dry in the sun. "How can you ever know if someone traded the stolen beaver pelts to him? You can't just ask him!"

"No," Suzette said slowly. A school of tiny minnows swam past her legs, tickling her skin. She hardly noticed. "I'll have to go to his camp and wait until he leaves, and then . . . see what I can find."

"Sneak into his camp?" Gabrielle stared. "Suzette, what if he catches you?"

"I won't let him catch me," Suzette said. Her voice was confident. She just wished her insides—the place in her stomach suddenly churning like a stormy lake—felt as certain.

I have made a decision," Papa said that evening. The family was gathered outside their *wiigwams,* once again listening to the distant singing and laughter from the *voyageurs'* camp. "Tomorrow morning, we will take down our lodge. We're going to cross the water again and make a summer camp on the mainland." He looked at Grandmother. "I hope you and Yellow Wing will join us. But I am speaking for my wife and daughters."

For a moment no one spoke. Grandmother's eyes widened. Mama nodded silently. Suzette, who was holding Charlotte, felt her jaw drop.

"Our trouble started before we even arrived," Papa pointed out. "Someone damaged our canoe. Then I'm accused of stealing. I've even lost my cross." He gestured to his waist, where his beautiful silver crucifix usually hung on the woven band. "Many signs that it's time to leave—"

"Oh, Papa, no!" Suzette couldn't hold the words inside.

"I know you love La Pointe, *mignonne,*" Papa said. "But there's a cloud hanging over this lodge. My friends ask me to sing and laugh with them, but I'm too troubled. And every time I pass Captain d'Amboise or one of the other fort men, I know they are thinking, 'Did Philippe do it? Did Philippe steal the furs?'" He shook his head. "No, it's better to be out of sight until the trouble blows over."

Suzette lay her cheek against Charlotte's dusting of black hair. Worry twisted her insides, and her thoughts bubbled like a kettle of maple sap at sugaring time. The only way to truly set matters right was to find the thief. Then Papa's name would be cleared and the trappers' competition could go on. But how could she find the thief if they were on the mainland?

"It might look worse if you leave now," Yellow Wing pointed out.

Papa shrugged. "How can it look worse? D'Amboise has already searched my lodge. He has insulted me. I have too much pride to stay here."

Grandmother spoke for the first time. "You're right. Yellow Wing and I will come with you."

"It won't be so bad," Yellow Wing added. "We will have the best fishing spots to ourselves."

Suzette was trying desperately to think of reasons that might convince Papa to stay. "But, Papa," she managed, "what about my lessons? Monsieur Roussain is terribly behind with his ledgers. The *voyageurs* brought so many new goods from Montréal . . . and he's got to get all the trappers' furs bundled and counted . . . and I promised I'd help him. I gave him my word. Can't we stay for just a short while longer? Please, Papa?"

"A'jawac," Grandmother said quietly. She thought Suzette was being disrespectful by arguing with her father. Suzette bowed her head, waiting.

Her papa took a long time to find his words. "Two days," he said finally. "Two suns. Then we leave for the mainland."

"*Eya,* Papa," she said, feeling a little wave of relief. But her thoughts were still tumbling. Two suns! That didn't leave her much time.

"Daughter," Mama said the next morning, after Papa and Yellow Wing had left the lodge, "Grandmother and I are going to gather cedar bark this morning. We'd be glad of your help." Women gathered the inner bark of cedar trees to make mats and bags, and more hands made the work easier.

But Suzette couldn't afford to lose any more time in tracking the thief. "Mama," she said hesitantly, "I'd be happy to help you. But Grandmother mentioned that she needed some bloodroot to dye quills with, and I thought

I'd look for some for her. And then I was going to help Monsieur Roussain . . ." Her voice trailed away, and she studied the pine needles at her feet. She didn't want to say more than she needed to.

Her mother regarded her. "Ah, Suzette," she said finally. "This has all been difficult for you, I know. Your father is a good man. Everything will come out well, I think."

"I think so too, Mama," Suzette said. She had to believe it.

"You may go. Try not to worry. The Spirit of the Woods will watch over you."

Suzette nodded. Mama had often told Suzette that the Spirit of the Woods would break a little branch and throw it in front of her in warning if she was ever about to walk into danger. It had reassured her when she was little, and it was comforting now. "*Eya*, Mama," she said. "I'll be careful."

Suzette packed some pemmican in a pouch. With an empty birch-bark *makak* on her hip to hold any bloodroot or food she might find, and tobacco to offer in thanks, she set off.

From the Ojibwe camp on the southwestern shore, Suzette headed north. Captain d'Amboise had said Jacques Dupré's camp was on the northeast end of the island, beyond Big Bay. La Pointe Island was long and narrow—more than a usual day's walk from end to end—but Big Bay was only partway toward the island's northeastern end. Suzette was traveling light, and her winter spent setting snares and helping her parents haul meat and pelts through deep snow had made her strong. She hoped to find the camp by midday.

A narrow trail led north through the forest of spruce, birch, and pine. She passed the area where she and Grandmother had once dug wild ginger, and the chokecherry trees the island women harvested every year. But soon she had left behind familiar landmarks.

The sun was high overhead by the time Suzette reached the sandy beach at Big Bay. She had often paddled here with Mama to cut bulrushes from the bog stretching inland from the bay, but now she looked out over the glittering waters of *Lac Supérieur,* which disappeared into the horizon. A tiny island jutted from the water like the fin on a trout. There were no canoes in sight.

"Now what?" she wondered, munching some pemmican. She guessed Dupré's camp was farther north. Beyond the beach the shoreline was rocky, and she jumped from boulder to boulder until she reached a tall rock wall rising straight from the lake. Then she found a faint trail that climbed the bluffs skirting the shore. Swallows swooped and dove near the water.

Suzette let her pace slow. She proceeded cautiously, alert for any sign that she was nearing the camp. She had been taught to walk silently and to use all of her senses to explore the forest. Her nose found the camp first: a faint whiff of stale smoke.

For a moment she stood rooted. What was she doing here? What would Mama say about her daughter creeping around the camp of an illegal trader? What would Dupré do if he found her? A gull called from overhead, as if laughing at her.

Just go on! Suzette ordered herself angrily. Taking a deep breath, she left the path and crept through the underbrush, following her nose. Finally she stopped, crouching behind an ancient white pine near a small clearing. She listened. Hearing nothing, she slowly peered around the trunk.

The camp was in a small opening among the trees, and looked deserted. It was not directly on the beach, as Suzette had imagined, but on the far side of the clearing. A path led down toward the lake. The fire pit looked cold. Faded tarps were tied against two trees to provide shelter for a jumble of bundles and crates, which she guessed were full of trade goods.

And behind them, almost hidden in the shadows, were several piles of pelts. Did she dare leave the safety of the trees? She hesitated, listening with every pore. She heard the wind sigh among the branches, and the faint hammer of a woodpecker. Nothing more.

She considered darting across the clearing, but it seemed safer to circle around through the woods, even though that meant skirting a thorny raspberry patch. It seemed to take forever! But finally she tiptoed up to the makeshift shelters.

What she had thought were piles of loose pelts were instead packed bales with a few stiff skins tossed on top. Suzette pawed through the loose hides desperately. No telltale beaver pelts with golden stripes. She chewed her lip. Should she try to open the big bales?

Her heart began to thump. Opening the packed furs would take time. She broke into a nervous sweat as she stepped away from the shelter for a moment, into the dappled sunshine beneath the forest canopy, listening—

Then the twig dropped in front of her.

Suzette froze, staring at the tiny bit of branch beside her moccasin. Her skin tingled. Perhaps it was no more than a twig knocked to the ground by a squirrel, but she was suddenly afraid. *Hide!* she thought, and at the same moment, she heard voices approaching from the lake path.

She looked around quickly for a hiding place. Only a thin strip of scrubby woods shielded her from the lakeshore. Most of the clearing was bounded by open spruce and pine forest. With no better choice, she darted to the raspberry thicket, slipping around the worst of the briars and ignoring the sting of those that plucked at her arms. She spied an ancient fallen tree among the undergrowth and dropped to the ground behind it just as two men came around a bend in the trail. Her body made no sound, but she misjudged the *makak*. It brushed against a dead branch, snapping off the tip.

"What was that?" a man said. He spoke French with

a heavy accent that Suzette didn't recognize. She pressed close to the ground, hardly daring to breathe.

"What was what? I didn't hear anything." The second man spoke fluent French.

"I heard something, Dupré."

Suzette's heart raced. Dupré? This was the man!

"You heard nothing more than a rabbit in the brush," the French voice—Dupré—said. "You're jumpy as a rabbit yourself, Mikail. Here. Hand me the flask. If you're going to stare at nothing, I might as well stop for a drink."

"This business makes me jumpy," Mikail said defensively. "This is not what I signed on for."

"Quit complaining. I pay well."

"But you didn't say that Baptiste would bring a French soldier to search the camp! I don't like soldiers. I want no more trouble with the law. You know that is why I left home for this godforsaken wilderness."

Baptiste and a French soldier had searched the camp? Captain d'Amboise must have made good on his promise of sending them to visit Dupré's camp. They must have paddled around the island the afternoon before.

"Nothing was found, was it? At least nothing they could prove was stolen?" Dupré gave a harsh laugh. "Don't worry so much. Those two striped beaver pelts are safe in the cave, and they'll bring good money."

Striped beaver pelts! Suzette wanted to whoop. Instead she pressed her cheek against the rotting wood, smelling the dank odors of moss and decay. She held her breath, willing Mikail and Dupré to say more.

"Come on," Dupré said. "We need to haul this last load over to Gull Rock and get it hidden away safe with the rest. Let's get going."

"Maybe you'll get more of those striped beaver pelts before we go back to Montréal," Mikail said hopefully. Then he grunted, as if swinging a heavy load to his back.

"There's one more of those to come in. But don't look for any more after that," Dupré scoffed. "Our man said they came from somewhere west of here. But don't worry, I tell you! Once we get back to Montréal, I'll make it worth your while . . ." The voices faded away.

Suzette waited to be sure the men were truly gone before emerging from her hiding place. Too late, she realized she should have tried to follow them. She crept toward the lake, keeping out of sight of anyone using the faint path, but by the time she reached the shore, there was no sign of the two men.

A flood of frustrated disappointment washed over her. Her whole body ached, and she realized that she had been clenching every muscle tight. Still, she was excited. She hadn't found the stolen furs or identified the thief. But she knew for sure now that the thief was trading with Jacques Dupré.

And the furs had been hidden in a cave, just as she had suspected. And since the men were taking these furs to be "safe with the rest," the cave must be near Gull Rock. But where *was* Gull Rock? She'd never heard of such a place. And who had brought the stolen furs to Dupré in the first place? Dupré had referred to "our man." Who was "our man"? Niskigwun? Big Nicolas? Or someone else?

She hadn't come up with any answers by the time she saw the French flag flying over the trading post and heard the shouts of boys playing *bagaadowe* nearby. The trail emerged from the forest near a back corner of the stockade. As she left the woods, Suzette could smell roasting venison. The afternoon was lengthening. She began to run lightly, anticipating whatever meal was waiting at her own lodge.

Then she rounded another corner of the stockade and stopped abruptly. Two soldiers were leading a man into the fort. She could tell by the way the soldiers held him that he was a prisoner. Captain d'Amboise and Roussain were with them. A small group of Ojibwe people and *voyageurs* stood back, watching.

Then Suzette got a better look, and her heart plummeted. The prisoner was Papa.

"*Non!*" she screamed, and launched toward the group. She caught up with them just inside the fort gate. She tried to reach Papa, but Captain d'Amboise caught her. "*Non!*" she cried over and over. "*Non,* let him go! It's not true!"

D'Amboise gave her a little shake. "Yes, it is. Now go home to your mother." He turned toward the crowd and raised his voice. "Go home! There is nothing more to see here."

Suzette tried again to reach her father—even just to look into his eyes. But the soldiers blocked her, and Papa's head hung low to his chest. He must have heard her. But he did not turn his head.

"It's not true," Suzette sobbed. She grabbed d'Amboise's arm, frantic to make him listen. "Papa didn't do it, I know he didn't do it—"

"Yes, he did!" d'Amboise shouted. "We have proof. Do you hear me? We have proof!"

CHAPTER 9
ARREST

The soldiers jerked Papa away. Suzette watched them disappear into one of the fort buildings with d'Amboise. The door slammed behind them. The onlookers wandered away, muttering to one another, looking at her. Suzette felt helpless as a snared rabbit.

"Suzette!" Monsieur Roussain had to shout her name before she realized he was standing beside her. "Come inside." The clerk pulled her toward the store. He had to turn a key in a big lock before they went inside, and he shut the door behind them—a sign of how shocking the day's events were. Roussain *never* closed the shop so early. That closed door seemed to slam in Suzette's heart.

Hot tears spilled down her cheeks. "Why did they arrest Papa?" she demanded, scrubbing at the tears with her fist. "What proof does Captain d'Amboise think he has?"

Roussain led her toward his stool. "Sit down. I'll tell you everything. I want you to hear it from me, not those telling tales outside." He took a deep breath. "This afternoon, two of our soldiers were cutting firewood on the interior of the island. They found a bundle of furs hidden behind a tree. That's not so unusual, but because of the theft, the soldiers brought them to me. There were a couple of rabbit pelts, and an otter. But there was also one beaver pelt. This is it."

The clerk pushed the pelt toward her. It lay fur-side down on the counter. The skin had been washed and scraped free of flesh and fat, stretched into a neat oval, and dried stiff as a slice of pine—just like any pelt. But Suzette's hand shook as she turned the skin over.

The animal had been trapped in deep winter—perhaps the moon of crusted snow—for the dark fur was lush and thick. Running down the middle of the pelt was something she'd never before seen: a golden streak. *There's one more of those pelts to come in,* Dupré had said . . .

Suzette shoved the pelt away as though it burned her fingers. "What of this?" she demanded. "Yes, it's one of the stolen furs. But you must listen to me!" Quickly she told him what she had overheard in Dupré's camp. "Dupré said he had two of the striped pelts already safe in some cave. And he said, 'There's one more of those to come in. But don't look for any more after that. Our man said they came from somewhere west of here . . .'" Suzette sputtered into silence. She hadn't said anything that would clear Papa. "Anyway, what does this pelt"—she gestured angrily—"have to do with Papa? Why should anyone believe *he* took it?"

"The soldiers found something with the pelts, dropped by the man who put them there." Roussain's eyes were sad as he opened his palm. Something small fell on the counter: a silver cross hanging from a band of fine blue, red, and yellow wool, finger-woven in an ornate lightning pattern.

Papa's crucifix. The one he had brought from Montréal, and kept on the band Mama had woven for him, hung at his waist.

"I recognized the cross. I had to tell the captain—"

"Papa *said* he had lost it," Suzette interrupted furiously. "Someone must have found it, and—"

"But there's more." Roussain formed the words as if with great effort. "I went with the captain and the soldiers to your family's lodge. At first your father denied everything. But when Captain d'Amboise began to question Yellow Wing, your father confessed—"

"I don't believe you!"

"Suzette, I was there! He said Yellow Wing had nothing to do with it. 'I'm your man,' he said. 'I'm the man you have been looking for.'"

Suzette felt tears come again. She jumped from the stool, pulled open the door, and ran. "Suzette, I'm sorry!" her friend called after her, but she didn't turn around.

It's all my fault. It's all my fault. The words pounded in her head as she ran from the fort, away from the camp, toward the lakeshore. Papa had stayed on the island because of her. If she hadn't begged to stay, if they had left the island, perhaps Papa wouldn't be locked up in some small room. Papa, who loved fresh air and open water and room to dance and sing!

Her lungs began to burn, and she stopped running. The distant call of a loon echoed over the lake and she wished her family could paddle away, follow that loon. She pictured her family: hurt, confused, angry. Perhaps Grandmother was telling Mama she shouldn't have married a French man . . .

Suzette wasn't ready to face them. *Gabrielle.* She'd find Gabrielle.

She slipped back around the fort to the Ojibwe camp. Fortunately, Gabrielle's lodge was not in sight of Suzette's own. She found Gabrielle's father painting new designs on his paddle, but he scrambled up when he saw her.

"Ah, Suzette," he said sadly, and she knew that he had already seen or heard what happened. "I don't believe these tales for a moment. None of your papa's old friends do, eh? When you see him, tell him we miss him around the fires at night."

"*Oui,* I'll tell him," she mumbled. "Is Gabrielle about?"

"Gabrielle took the little ones to the beach to play."

"*Merci,*" Suzette said in thanks. She found her friend

sitting on a rock at the lakeshore, watching her two younger sisters wade in the shallows. "Gabrielle—"

"I heard what happened," her friend interrupted. Her dark eyes were sad.

Suzette sat down beside her, avoiding her gaze. "*It's not true.* Papa could not have done this bad thing."

"Suzette . . ." Gabrielle hesitated. "I know your papa is a good man. But he was desperate to win the competition, wasn't he? He wanted to keep your family together—"

"*No.*" The word struck like flint on a fire steel. "He did not do this."

Gabrielle rubbed a bone of driftwood nervously. "*Eya.* I believe you. But—but why did he tell Captain d'Amboise he was the one? People are saying that he said—"

"I *know* what he said! Monsieur Roussain told me that he—he confessed." It was hard even to say the word. *Why* had Papa said he was the one? "I don't know why Papa would say such a thing, Gabrielle. But there must be an explanation."

"I'm sure there is," Gabrielle said loyally, although she still looked uncertain.

Suzette drew a deep breath, sifting sand through her fingers. "And there's even more." She told Gabrielle about Papa's crucifix. "It looks bad, I know. But I know my papa. He is *not* a thief!"

"Can you talk to him?"

"Captain d'Amboise has locked him up. I saw him just

as they led him inside the fort, but he wouldn't look at me."
Suzette would not admit aloud that her father had looked
ashamed, his head hung low. "I guess Captain d'Amboise
will keep Papa locked up for a short time, while they ask
him questions. But then . . ." She swallowed hard. "You
know what the captain said. We'll have to leave La Pointe.
And I don't know where we'll go, Gabrielle." A sudden lump
in her throat choked off her words. If Papa was banished,
would she ever see Gabrielle again?

"Oh, Suzette." Gabrielle bowed her head, but not before
Suzette saw tears glistening on her dark lashes. Suzette
looked over the lake, blinking back her own tears. Beyond
the splashing girls, the water moved restlessly, fading into
the horizon. The sun was just starting to sink in the western
sky. Just as all her hopes for the future were sinking . . .

No. Suzette pounded her fist on her knee, unwilling to
admit defeat. "Someone is doing this to us," she said. "I
don't know who. Or why. But *someone* is trying to get Papa
in trouble. *Someone* damaged Papa's canoe. And . . . *someone*
found Papa's silver cross and left it with the stolen furs."

"But how could that person have known that the soldiers would find them?"

Suzette chewed that over. "It's not so hard, really. The
soldiers have been cutting firewood. They don't go any
farther than they have to. All someone had to do was see
where they left off cutting one day. It wouldn't be hard to
guess where they'd be the next day."

Her friend nodded thoughtfully.

"And, Gabrielle, I haven't even told you what else happened today!" Quickly Suzette described Dupré's camp and what she had overheard. "And so they *are* hiding the rest of the stolen furs in a cave," she finished. "Did your brother tell you anything about caves? Is there a cave on the island?"

"He said no—unless some of the rocks along the shore form a small cave."

"But where?" Suzette persisted. Almost all of the island's shoreline was rocky! She clenched her fists in frustration.

Gabrielle shook her head. "That's all he knew about caves. He did tell me something else, though. About Niskigwun." Gabrielle looked over her shoulder, then leaned closer. "His wife was a Dakota!"

"*What?*" Suzette could hardly believe it. The Dakota people to the west had always been enemies of the Ojibwe.

Gabrielle nodded excitedly. "Think about it! Niskigwun was married to one of our enemies!"

"Niskigwun is a bad one," Suzette agreed slowly. "But that doesn't prove he's the thief." She thought for a moment. "Gabrielle, I have to find Dupré's cave."

"What can you learn there?"

Suzette didn't have a good answer ready. "Maybe Dupré keeps records, like Monsieur Roussain's ledgers. Or maybe once I find the cave, I can hide and see who comes to do business with Dupré. I don't know! But anything is better than sitting still while Captain d'Amboise holds Papa prisoner." Suzette took a deep breath, determined to follow the only plan she could think of. "If your brother's right, the cave must be somewhere along the shoreline. It seems to me that the easiest way to begin searching for it is from the water. Will you come canoeing with me tomorrow?"

Gabrielle hesitated. "I want to help, but . . . Dupré sounds like a dangerous man."

"We won't get in any trouble," Suzette promised recklessly. "We'll be careful. Please, Gabrielle." She held her breath. She needed Gabrielle to help paddle.

"Well, I'll have to ask Mama, but she'll probably say yes." Gabrielle turned and studied the shoreline. "What direction will we go in? This is a big island. We can't paddle all the way around it tomorrow."

Suzette tipped her head to one side, considering. Dupré and Mikail's camp was on the east side of the island. But the island was narrow, and the men were no doubt strong and well used to hauling or paddling heavy loads for long distances. The cave at Gull Rock could be anywhere.

In frustration she picked up a stone, ready to hurl it into the water. Something made her pause. She turned it over in her palm. It was a small stone, rippling red and gray, smooth as polished wood. She had a sudden memory of herself as a young child, and her Ojibwe grandfather telling her that beach stones were once rough but had been worn smooth by the waves. "It can't be!" she had protested. "The stone is hard, and the water soft. It's the water that gives." Grandfather shook his head. "Keep this stone," he said, handing Suzette the pebble. "Let it remind you that water can wear away stone. The water needs only patience, and persistence."

Patience and persistence, Suzette thought now. She had kept the pebble, tucked safely in a fringed pouch that held her most treasured possessions. *I'll carry it with me tomorrow,* she thought. *If water can wear away stone, I can figure out who is doing these terrible things.*

"I don't know which direction we should paddle," she admitted. "But I'll figure something out. Now, I should go. Mama doesn't even know I'm back."

"I'll walk with you," Gabrielle said. "The girls have been playing long enough. Aai!" She got the two girls' attention and waited for a moment while they scampered about for a few last minutes to test their sister's patience.

Suzette was just about to tell her friend that she couldn't wait any longer when she saw a canoe glide around the point from the east and angle toward the beach. As the canoe drew near, Gabrielle hissed something under her breath. Suzette froze, staring.

There were two men in the canoe—Niskigwun and Big Nicolas.

It was a quiet night on the island. Even the *voyageurs* were still, as if they could not sing knowing one of their own was in trouble. In Suzette's lodge the silence was terrible.

Suzette tried to take comfort from her resolve to keep searching for the real thief, but the pained look in Mama's eyes made it hard to think of anything except Papa's banishment. Captain d'Amboise had told Mama that Papa would be held in the fort for fourteen suns. When he was released, he would have to leave La Pointe. Mama did not say what would happen to the family then, and Suzette was afraid to ask. There was no answer she wanted to hear.

She tossed fitfully on her blankets, tormented by her thoughts. *We will have nowhere to go,* she thought. *We will be welcome nowhere.* She felt like a baby sparrow fallen from the nest. What would they do? Wander by themselves into the western country, where they would be strangers? Would Papa leave them after all and go back to Montréal? Either way, Mama and Grandmother and Yellow Wing could perhaps make a home for themselves somewhere among the Ojibwe—they could lose themselves, blend in among the others.

But where was she to go? A black-haired, blue-eyed girl who was both French and Ojibwe—and neither?

CHAPTER 10
TRAPPED

Everyone was up at dawn, when the first songs of chickadees and warblers rang through the trees. The morning was gray and damp. Mama began preparing flatbread outside as if every move took enormous effort. Yellow Wing sat smoking his pipe in a patch of weak light angling through the pines, his shoulders hunched. When Mama offered him some flatbread, he shook his head, then got up and walked away. *He is ashamed of Papa*, Suzette thought. She was eager to leave the *wiigwam* behind.

"Mama, I told Gabrielle we could go paddling today," she said, careful not to meet her mother's eye.

"Paddling, Granddaughter?" Grandmother asked. "At such a time as this?"

"I need something to do," Suzette said quickly. "I can't just sit here and—and think. I promised Gabrielle. May I go?"

Suzette turned to Mama and saw that her eyes were shining with tears. Suzette had never seen her mother cry, and the very idea frightened her. Mama was the pine pitch that held her family together. *Maybe I should stay,* she thought guiltily. *Maybe I shouldn't leave Mama—*

But Mama decided for her. "You may go," she said quietly. "We need new bulrushes. It's early, but you may be able to find some in the bog at Big Bay."

Suzette hadn't expected a chore, but she didn't argue. She went back into the lodge and grabbed some dried fish and cranberries to fill the hole in her belly, and a knife to cut the bulrushes. Then she rummaged among her belongings until she found her pouch. It was made from a beaver pelt and decorated with fringe. The pebble Grandfather had given her was inside. So was the silver crucifix Papa had given her when she was small, and a little beaded turtle her mother had sewn. They were Suzette's most cherished possessions, and she wanted them with her as she searched for Dupré's camp. Back outside, she tied the knife and her pouch around her waist.

"A'jawac, what are you doing?" Grandmother was busy unraveling a new wool blanket from the trading post. Suzette knew she would dye the wool and weave it into something else—a sash, perhaps, or a gathering bag. Grandmother rarely accepted a French trade item without changing it in some way to suit her. She was wearing an earbob made of a silver thimble Papa had given her to sew with.

Suzette felt a wave of irritation. Why couldn't Grandmother just accept things—and people—as they were? Why did the French bother her so? Suzette struggled to hide her annoyance as she answered. "Getting ready to go, Grandmother. I want to take my pouch with me."

"Wait." It was a command. Suzette sighed as Grandmother put her blanket aside and disappeared into her own *wiigwam*.

Suzette was fidgeting by the time Grandmother emerged. "You'd be wise not to be in such a hurry," Grandmother said. She reached for her granddaughter's hand, placed something on Suzette's palm, and closed her fingers around it. "Carry this in your bag. It will bring a happy outcome to your difficulties."

Suzette looked at the shriveled twig in her hand. Grandmother's gift was a piece of dried root from a wild pea plant—the traditional Ojibwe charm for bringing success to someone anxious about a task. The charm seemed as old as Grandmother.

Then she noticed Grandmother's waiting eyes. Suzette felt ashamed. No wonder Grandmother worried about French influences! No Ojibwe girl was raised to be impatient or disrespectful to her elders. "Thank you, Grandmother," she said quietly, slipping the root into her pouch. "I will carry it with me."

Suzette took her canoe to the beach. Mist was drifting over the lake, and the water looked dark and cold.

She put the canoe down carefully just as someone appeared from a side path along the shore, carrying a spear and a basket holding several flopping trout. It was Niskigwun's son, Two Fish.

Suzette hadn't seen him face-to-face since they'd left the mainland. His taunt rang in her head. *Blue Eyes! Blue Eyes!* The reminder made her feel sick, and she froze. Should she speak to him? Turn away?

Before she could decide, he stopped in front of her and opened his mouth to speak. She couldn't bear to hear another insult, and she cut him off. "Dakota boy!" she hissed. "You are an ugly boy. Your mother was one of our enemies."

Two Fish pulled his lips together, covering his broken tooth. Then he turned and walked away. Suzette stared after him, feeling cold and small.

When Gabrielle joined her, the girls settled their paddles into the canoe. They were about to carry it into the water when someone called. "Suzette!"

Baptiste and Monsieur Roussain were walking along the shore. "Suzette, *bonjour*," the clerk said carefully.

"*Bonjour,* Monsieur Roussain, Baptiste." Suzette forced

herself to look both men in the eye. It wasn't their fault
Papa was locked up. "What are you doing here so early?"

"I spend all my days inside the store," Roussain said.
"I often walk here early in the morning. Where are you
girls headed?"

"I'm trying to catch the *real* thief." Suzette wanted
them to know that she didn't believe her papa was guilty.

But she wished she had kept silent as Baptiste squatted
to look her in the eye. "Suzette, I don't think that's a
good idea," he said gently. "I told you before, you should
give that up. The thief is probably a rough man. Doesn't
your mother have enough problems without you getting
into trouble?"

The concern in his voice gave Suzette pause. She had
never seen Baptiste worry about anyone! Baptiste was
older than she, and wise. She knew she should listen to
him. But what choice did she have? "We're just looking,"
she said slowly. "We won't get into any trouble."

He still looked worried. "Come to me, if you find anything. I'll help you."

Roussain was worried too. "Should you two girls be
heading out alone? The lake waters can be dangerous, and
it smells like rain."

Suzette shrugged. "We're not afraid of rain."

Her tutor shook his head. "Suzette, no good French girl
would run wild as you do. Remember your French blood."

How could she forget it? "We'll be fine," she called as

the girls splashed into the lake with the canoe and stepped inside. "We'll keep close to shore. Don't worry!"

Suzette sat in the bow and used her paddle to help point the canoe east. "Mama asked me to cut bulrushes at Big Bay," she said over her shoulder to Gabrielle. "And that takes us in the direction we saw Niskigwun and Big Nicolas coming from." She had looked in their canoe last evening as the men paddled in. It had been empty— no fish or fishing gear—and that made her even more suspicious. Why had they been out paddling together?

Suzette dipped her paddle with long, even strokes. The water was so clear she could see the rocky lake bottom, an occasional fish. As the girls paddled past the point, leaving the fort and the Ojibwe camp behind, Suzette was surprised to see Yellow Wing wading waist-deep into the cold lake. As she and Gabrielle eased the canoe toward him, he waved. "Where are you girls going?"

"Out to cut bulrushes," Suzette said quickly. "Mama asked me to. What are you doing?"

Yellow Wing lifted a fish trap from the water. It was the one he had been repairing, designed so fish could swim in a narrow opening at one end without being able to turn around and swim back out. "I set this last night," he said, and carefully opened a gate on the top of his trap. With a nod of satisfaction, he lifted a large speckled lake trout through the gate. It twisted in his hands. "Thank you for feeding my family," Yellow Wing murmured to the trout, then turned to the girls. "This fish swam in the opening and tried all night to get back out the same way. He never thought to try to leave through the top."

"You're a good fisherman, Yellow Wing," Suzette told him. His success meant a meal of fresh trout would be waiting for her return.

"If they let me see Philippe later, I'll tell him," Yellow Wing said bitterly. "I'll tell him that at least he doesn't need to fear that his wife and daughters will go hungry." Then he added more gently, "Don't worry about that, Suzette."

Suzette repeated his comforting words in her head as they moved on. Yellow Wing was a good provider. When the sturgeon spawned each spring, he speared more fish than almost anyone, and the family's best winter feast had come after he killed a moose—

She stopped paddling abruptly and turned around. "Gabrielle! I know why Papa told Captain d'Amboise he was the thief!"

Gabrielle looked startled. "Why?"

"Because they were questioning Yellow Wing! Yellow Wing was with Papa the night the furs were stolen. Captain d'Amboise might have locked them *both* up. Since the soldiers found Papa's crucifix, and there was no chance they'd believe *he* was innocent, Papa wanted to be sure Yellow Wing went free. So there would be someone left to look after the rest of us."

That had to be it. Suzette felt a flood of relief so strong

she wanted to whoop, or cry, or laugh out loud. Everything else could be blamed on whoever had truly stolen the furs. The one thing she hadn't understood, the part that had hurt the most, was hearing that Papa had confessed. Now she knew why he had done it. He had done it to protect his family.

Suzette lifted her paddle and began to stroke with fresh energy. "Come on, Gabrielle," she called. "I want to find that cave."

All that morning the girls paddled along the eastern side of the island, eyeing the rocky shore as they made their way toward Big Bay. Each time they spied a shadowy nook among the rocks, they paused to get a good look. Several times they beached the canoe and scrambled up to see if some slight overhang might be a cave entrance, but they found nothing. They stopped to look at every rock where gulls gathered, with no better results.

"This is getting us nowhere," Suzette admitted finally, when the day was half gone. They'd passed Big Bay, and the spot where Suzette had found Dupré's camp, without finding anything.

Gabrielle scooped some lake water to her mouth for a drink. "Suzette, the clouds are getting lower, and grayer. We should head back before the rain comes in."

Suzette opened her mouth to protest, then closed it.

"I'll come back out with you after the bad weather," Gabrielle added. "I promise."

Suzette swallowed her disappointment, heartened by her friend's loyalty. "All right," she said. "Let's go back to the bog at Big Bay. I can't go home without cutting some bulrushes. It won't take long."

Soon the girls had a good armload of bulrushes lying in the canoe, ready for Mama to clean and dye and weave with basswood fibers into sturdy sitting mats. Suzette paused to munch some dried cranberries, and let her gaze drift across the water to the tiny, fin-shaped island that she had noticed the day she found Dupré's camp. It was about half as far away as the mainland. Suddenly she stopped chewing. "Gabrielle, look! Maybe *that's* Gull Rock!" She pointed to a rock outcrop on the little island that looked just like the head of a gull.

Gabrielle considered. "It could be."

"It would be an easy paddle from Dupré's camp. Let's go take a look!" Suzette reached for her paddle.

Gabrielle didn't move. "We can't paddle over there! Papa has told me never to cross open water on the great lake without an adult along."

Suzette hesitated. Hadn't she heard the same command? She'd never been away from the shore without Papa or Mama or Yellow Wing. She chewed her lip, staring across to the little island. "I'm sure we can do it."

"But a storm may be coming," Gabrielle argued. "Let's ask my papa or one of the fort men to paddle us over."

"We're strong," Suzette said stubbornly. She didn't

want to ask for help. What if no one believed her? What if some of the men did investigate and found nothing? Maybe they would be angry and think she was lying to help her papa! "We can do it."

"Dupré's camp is just north of here. What if he sees us paddling to the island?"

"I don't think it's likely. Please, Gabrielle."

Gabrielle stared at the rock shaped like a gull head. "All right," she said finally. "Just a quick look, though, Suzette. One quick look, then we head for home."

"Yes. One quick look." Suzette was already drawing her paddle straight through the water toward the bow, turning the canoe away from La Pointe Island.

Once away from shore, the girls were paddling into a stronger wind. Suzette felt a flicker of apprehension down her backbone. What would happen if Dupré *did* spot them heading toward Gull Rock? She couldn't help looking back over her shoulder.

The crossing took longer than she had expected. When they finally reached waist-deep water again, Suzette slipped over the side, into the cold water, to walk the birch-bark canoe into the shallows. She looked around carefully as she towed the canoe toward a narrow beach. She didn't want to stumble over Dupré and Mikail! But no other canoes were in sight.

Boulders and downed trees, evidence of a lake storm's fury, littered the beach and steep, rocky slope beyond.

Cliffs towered over her head on either side of the beach, jutting straight into the water. A few scrubby pines clung stubbornly to the rocks, their roots anchored in crevices and their gnarled branches leaning over the water. High above Suzette's head, a tangled thicket of stunted juniper covered the island's crest. On such a small island, beaten by the wind on all sides, no tree grew full and tall.

From the beach, Suzette spied a dark opening near a boulder on the slope above. "That might be the cave!" she breathed, pointing. Gabrielle held the canoe near shore as Suzette scrambled up to look.

She had to climb over several downed trees near the opening. Gusts of cold wind pierced her damp leggings, reminding her that Gabrielle was probably shivering and impatient below. She cocked her head, listening to make sure Dupré was not inside, but she heard nothing except a gull crying in the distance. Stooping, she peered into the opening. She could barely make out the walls of a shadow-filled cavern. "It *is* a cave!" she whispered. Surely this was Dupré's hiding place!

She climbed back down to the shore. "I found the cave! But I think we should hide our canoe before we go inside."

"Why? You said we'd just take a peek and head back." Gabrielle cast a nervous look toward La Pointe.

Suzette shook her head. "We shouldn't take chances. I wouldn't want Dupré to spot it."

The girls struggled to carry the fragile canoe over the rocks to the far side of the island, where it couldn't be seen by anyone approaching from La Pointe. As soon as it was safely hidden beneath some pines, they scrambled back over the rough terrain and made their way to the cave.

Suzette's skin prickled as she led the way through the low entrance. What would she find? *Please, please, let it be something that will help Papa!* Once inside, she was able to stand, but it was hard to see anything in the dim light leaking through the low opening. The air smelled dank and musty, and the ceiling—low enough to touch with her hand—seemed to press down on her. Suzette wasn't used to being confined, and she shivered. Did Papa feel this way, locked away at the fort?

Thinking of Papa stiffened her determination. She blinked as her eyes adjusted to the gloom. Slowly she made out barrels and untidy bales of furs piled against the rock wall. Whole bales! Dupré must have been doing a lot of illegal trading. The cave was small, maybe the size of three *wiigwams,* and the jumble stretched from wall to wall.

"We've found the hiding place!" Suzette whispered. "It's Dupré's cache, I know it."

"It must be! We must go back and tell Captain d'Amboise!"

"Wait, Gabrielle. I want to see if there's anything here that will help Papa."

"Like what? Come on, Suzette. Let's go."

"Just a moment more." Suzette ran her hands over the nearest bundles and barrels, wishing she had better light. If only she'd brought a torch! *There must be something here to tell us who the thief is,* she thought, drumming her fingers on one of the parcels. She felt a few tiny trade beads under her fingertips and played with them absently while she tried to think.

But nothing helpful came to mind. "You're right," she sighed finally. "What did I expect to find, a neat ledger like Monsieur Roussain keeps, listing who brought the stolen furs? We should just leave—"

Suddenly the sound of a man's voice echoed from the beach below. Suzette's blood turned cold as the great lake itself.

Gabrielle clutched her arm. "Let's run—"

"No, they'd see us!" Suzette hissed. "Hide!" She grabbed Gabrielle's hand and darted to the back of the cave. The girls crouched behind two barrels and a fur bale. Suzette tried to squeeze herself into the ground, hoping desperately that in the shadows, they'd be invisible from the cave entrance.

"They must have seen us paddling over!" Gabrielle whispered.

Suzette didn't want to face that possibility. "Maybe they're just bringing in another load," she whispered back. "We'll wait until they're gone again, then leave."

It sounded good. But the cave was small. If the men

were here to load these goods into their canoe, or if they lit torches . . . Suzette's skin felt damp and clammy. Fear twisted in her belly.

She closed her eyes and waited. Gabrielle clutched one of her hands so hard it hurt. Suzette slid her free hand into her pouch. Her fingers found the pebble . . . the turtle . . . the cross . . . the pea root. She gathered them all into her palm and squeezed, desperate for reassurance.

Footsteps sounded on the rocks outside, accompanied by voices raised in anger. Suzette's heart pounded as she recognized Dupré's voice. "*Imbécile!*" he snapped. "You left this morning without hiding the entrance!"

"It is not my fault!" That was Mikail's accented French. "You *told* me to hurry back. Why must you yell at me?"

"Because you deserve it."

Suzette could tell that Dupré had entered the cave, for his voice rang loud and harsh in the enclosed space. She held her breath, every muscle clenched tight. *Go away, go away* . . . The silence that followed seemed to last forever.

"That's strange," Dupré finally muttered. "It doesn't look like anyone's been here. But I thought sure I saw a canoe near the shore below."

"All you saw was a shadow. We paddled over here for nothing," Mikail complained. His voice was muffled, as if he was waiting outside.

"For nothing? I found out you forgot to hide the entrance, didn't I? What if one of the fort men had spotted this place? What if we came back tomorrow to load the canoes and begin the paddle back to Montréal, and found that the soldiers had taken all of our furs?" Dupré's voice faded too. Suzette drew a tiny breath of relief as she imagined him stooping and leaving the cave.

She heard Mikail's muffled voice, then Dupré's harsh one. "Oh, shut up! And help me with this—"

Suzette heard something being dragged, a branch snapping, Mikail muttering an oath. The men were hauling the downed trees across the small entrance to the cave. Horror washed away the trickle of relief she'd felt. *They were barricading the cave!*

Finally the noise and commotion ceased. The men's voices faded away. "Suzette?" Gabrielle whispered. "Are they gone?"

"I think so. But let's wait, give them plenty of time."

Still holding hands, they waited. The sound of their breathing echoed in the deepening gloom. "Now," Suzette whispered finally. "They must be away from the island by now."

The girls stumbled to their feet and made their way toward the entrance. Only a few faint shafts of light angled through the branches of the downed trees blocking the opening.

"Maybe we can push them back," Suzette said. On their knees, the two girls tried to shove the nearest tree away. The pine trunk was whorled with branches, broken now, that stabbed at their arms and faces. Suzette finally managed to find a clear spot on the trunk for her shoulder. Pushing her heels into the dirt, she shoved with all her might. "Help me, Gabrielle!"

"I'm trying!" Gabrielle was on her belly now, straining against the barricade.

Nothing moved.

"It's no good. They must have braced the trees between rocks," Suzette said finally, sinking back on her haunches.

She was breathless. Her face stung where a branch had whipped it, and one finger was bleeding. She stared at the barricade, facing the hard truth for the first time.

They were trapped.

CHAPTER 11
ACROSS STORMY WATERS

"What will happen to us?" Gabrielle whispered. "Our families won't know where to look for us."

"And what will happen when Dupré and Mikail return?" Suzette echoed. "What will they do when they find us here?"

There was no answer. Suzette could smell freedom through the branches blocking their way. It smelled of earth, of the lake, of the nearing storm. She was desperate to break free and fill her lungs with it all.

Think! she commanded herself. She tried to focus on what they should do next, but her mind whirled with the conversation she'd overheard. Dupré and Mikail were planning to load their furs and begin paddling back to Montréal tomorrow morning. Once they left, she would never have a way to prove her father's innocence! Only Dupré and Mikail could say who had *really* stolen the pelts from the trading post.

"Oh!" Gabrielle's voice caught in a sob as she struggled against the barricade. Guilt crashed over Suzette. What had she done? Gotten into terrible trouble, and taken her friend along with her! *You are responsible for this,* Suzette told herself. *Now you must find a way to solve the problem.*

She took a deep breath, trying to think calmly. For solace she let her fingers slide back into her beaver-skin pouch. She touched her treasures, soothed by the memory of each gift. Grandmother, Grandfather, Mama, and Papa—each had given something to protect her, to make her strong. The reminder made her feel that her family was with her, helping her. Only Yellow Wing wasn't represented. Then she realized that Yellow Wing had given her his own gift that morning. She smiled faintly, remembering the words he had spoken as he stood beside the fish trap . . .

Suddenly, Suzette scrambled to her feet. "We're doing this wrong," she told Gabrielle. "We're acting like Yellow Wing's trout! We already know we can't get out the way we got in. We need to see if there's another way out."

Cautiously, Suzette began to explore the dark cave, moving her fingers along the rock walls. "There's nothing here," Gabrielle said doubtfully, but she joined the search. The girls pulled the heavy fur bales and barrels away from the rock walls so they could check every crack and cranny.

Finally they gave up in defeat. "What now?" Gabrielle asked. Suzette could just make out her friend slumped against a fur bale in the dim light near the entrance.

"I don't know. Not yet." Suzette felt a cold breeze stir through the musty cave. The storm was finally unleashing itself over the island. A moment later she smelled rain, heard the drops pounding the ground outside. *Think, Suzette. Think . . .*

The fish trap.

"I've got another idea," she said. "Let's try the ceiling."

Starting at the entrance, the girls felt along the ceiling, slowly making their way toward the back of the cave. Suzette's fingers grew raw as she slid them along the cold stone—sometimes rough, sometimes smooth, always unyielding. In the darkness, she stumbled on the uneven floor. Her shoulders began to ache.

At the cave's highest point, near the back, Suzette could no longer reach the ceiling. She climbed on a barrel but felt it wobble as she tried to stand. "Gabrielle, come help me. I need you to hold the barrel."

Carefully, she reached upward again. As her fingers moved along the rock, a few grains of dirt sifted onto her face. Suddenly something firm but pliable brushed her fingers. She jerked her hand away. Taking a deep breath, she found it again. Recognition dawned. "Gabrielle, it's a tree root!" she cried. She scrabbled with both hands. "There's a place here that's not stone. It's earth!"

Suzette had the knife she'd used to cut bulrushes tucked in her belt, and Gabrielle found a rough stone near the cave entrance. They shoved a second barrel next to the first for Gabrielle to stand on, and began to scrape above their heads.

Dirt rained down on their faces and hair. Every so often they had to lower their arms and rest their aching shoulders. "We're not getting anywhere," Suzette finally cried in frustration, cradling a scraped knuckle.

"Don't stop," Gabrielle said, scraping hard. "This is the only chance we have."

It seemed as if the sun had time to rise and set and rise again before Suzette's knife poked through to the surface. She wiggled the knife in the narrow hole. "We're through, Gabrielle!" she cried.

The soil came away more easily then, in rain-dampened clumps. Suzette used her knife to saw through several smaller roots, showering more dirt around them. Finally she felt cold raindrops spatter her face. "Rain, Gabrielle! I can feel it!" She squinted at the small hole they'd clawed above their heads. "I think I can squeeze through. Just give me a foot up—"

Then she stopped and looked at her friend. Suzette's whole body quivered with longing to be out of that dark place. *This is your fault,* she reminded herself. She cupped her hands. "Here. You go first."

Gabrielle didn't hesitate before stepping lightly into Suzette's hands with one moccasined foot. On their first try, the barrel tipped over, dumping them to the cave floor. "Let me try again," she gasped. Straining to bear her friend's weight, Suzette watched Gabrielle's hands disappear through the hole, then her head. "Oooh!" Gabrielle wheezed, struggling to force her shoulders through the narrow opening. Suzette fought to keep her balance as she pushed from below. Then Gabrielle grunted, and with a sudden burst, she was through. Her feet disappeared, and gray light shafted through the hole.

Suzette felt a stab of abandonment. "Gabrielle!" she shouted. "Pull me up!"

This was harder. Gabrielle gripped Suzette's hands and pulled. For a long, painful moment, Suzette hung suspended, kicking her feet in the air, while Gabrielle tried to haul her through. Suzette's arms scraped against the sides. A root gouged her face. Mud was in her mouth, rain in her eyes. "You're slipping!" Gabrielle gasped. Suzette twisted frantically, shoving her shoulders through, then strained to plant one elbow on the ground. She fought with every muscle, refusing to fall back into the hole below. Another root dug into her ribs. Finally she managed to brace both elbows on solid ground. Gabrielle reached under Suzette's arms and pulled.

And she was free. She rolled away from the hole, suddenly slashed by driving rain. Gabrielle flopped beside her, breathing heavily, covered with mud. They were bruised and battered and Suzette began to laugh. "Thank you, Yellow Wing. And thank you, Gabrielle! We made it out! We did it!"

"We did it!" Gabrielle echoed. "I didn't think we'd ever get out of there." And she laughed too.

After a few moments, Suzette sat up and looked around. They were on top of the rocky bluff. The distant mainland was entirely veiled in mist. La Pointe Island was no more than a faint shadow. The sky was low and gray, the rain pouring down. The great lake was gray too, restless, choppy with white-capped waves. The last bits of Suzette's laughter died away.

Gabrielle was looking across the lake too. "We'll have to wait out the storm before heading back," she said quietly.

Suzette knew the danger of canoeing in such weather, but how else could she save Papa? "We've already lost so much time, Gabrielle!" she protested. "We've *got* to get back to the post before Dupré leaves for Montréal tomorrow! If we don't leave soon, we might have to spend the night here—"

"I'd rather spend the night here than drown!"

"Do you want to be here when those men come back in the morning?"

Gabrielle hesitated. She shoved a strand of dripping black hair away from her face.

"*Please,* Gabrielle! If Captain d'Amboise and Baptiste can catch those men, maybe they can make Dupré say who traded the striped beaver pelts to him."

"What makes you think Dupré will tell?"

"I don't *know* if he will. But I don't have any other ideas left! If Dupré paddles back to Montréal, I'll never be able to prove that Papa didn't steal those furs. Captain d'Amboise will keep him locked up for thirteen more suns, then send us all away." Her voice began to tremble. "And we have no place to go, Gabrielle. No place to go."

Gabrielle wiped cold rain from her face as she stared across the water to La Pointe. "Do you really think we can make it across?"

Suzette reached down. Her pouch was still in place, tied onto her belt. She reached inside and fingered her treasures: the stone, the crucifix, the turtle, the root. "Yes," she said finally. "We're both strong. We can do it."

Gabrielle rubbed her arms with her hands.

She still isn't sure, Suzette thought desperately. Making an effort to be heard above the wind and rain, she forced out words almost too unbearable to say. "What I'm most afraid of is that Papa will have to go back to Montréal, and Mama will have to stay here . . . and they'll make me pick which I'm going to be. French or Ojibwe." Tears burned her eyes, blurring with raindrops. "Oh, Gabrielle, what if they make me choose?"

For a long moment, Gabrielle didn't move or speak. Then she got up and began picking her way down the rain-slick hill toward the spot where they'd hidden the canoe.

Suzette jumped up and followed carefully down the rocky slope, hanging on to the gnarled pine trees. The girls didn't speak again until the canoe was in the water and they'd stepped inside.

"Paddling will keep us warm," Suzette called. "And we'll have a hot meal waiting. Think about that."

Gabrielle didn't answer. Suzette pointed the canoe toward La Pointe Island, bent her head against the driving rain, and began to paddle.

Suzette was strong. She had been out with Papa in stormy waters, and paddled on inland rivers where currents tried to decide where the canoe should go. But she'd never paddled like this before. The waves tossed the fragile canoe like a leaf in a stream. The wind tried to push them off course. Suzette paddled with the force of her whole body, straining, leaning, pushing.

From time to time she glanced up, checking to make sure they were still on course. But she didn't let herself think about how far they had to go, how slowly they were progressing. Finally she stopped thinking altogether and gave in to the rhythm. *Stroke, lift. Stroke, lift.* She ignored the ache in her bruised hands. Ignored the fire growing in her neck, along her shoulders, down her arms. Ignored her icy feet, soaked in the rainwater pooled at the bottom of the canoe. Ignored the fear gnawing at her belly. *Stroke, lift. Stroke, lift.*

The gray sky had deepened almost to charcoal before Suzette sensed a lessening in the struggle. She dared a look and saw the shoreline of La Pointe emerging from the mist, each rock and tree a wonderful sight. "Gabrielle, we're almost there!" Suzette called. Somehow she found the strength to keep paddling until the canoe was bobbing a stone's throw from shore.

Gabrielle put her paddle down and slumped forward. Suzette held her blade in the water, keeping the canoe pointed away from the rocks, and rested too. But they weren't home yet. Should they keep paddling along the shore toward the fort and the Ojibwe camp? Or beach the canoe and wait until dawn? She wasn't sure. And now that she'd stopped paddling, she didn't know if she could start again.

A confusing flicker from the south caught her attention. Then she recognized a torch. Someone was shouting their names. A canoe slid from the shadows.

It was Gabrielle's papa and Yellow Wing.

The other canoe pulled alongside theirs. "Thank God!" Gabrielle's father cried. "We've looked everywhere for you!"

In the flickering light of the torch, Yellow Wing's face was drawn. "Suzette. Oh, Suzette, I'm so glad we've found you."

"Not Suzette," she mumbled. Grandmother's voice quavered in her memory: *I named you because of a dream, a dream of you paddling across stormy waters.* "Not Suzette," she said again. "Today, my name is A'jawac."

Chapter 12
Purple Beads

The men paddled the hungry, shivering girls back to the beach below Fort La Pointe. Suzette had never been so happy to see the dark fort loom out of the shadows. A few stubborn campfires flickered through the trees. Near the beach, several *voyageurs* had strung a tarp in the pines and were sitting around a fire beneath it, singing one of their sad songs softly in harmony. The rain had tapered off to a drizzle.

Before Gabrielle and her papa disappeared toward their lodge, Suzette captured her friend in a French-style hug. "Thank you, Gabrielle," she whispered. "*Miigwech. Merci.*" She felt guilty for putting her friend through such an ordeal.

But Gabrielle hugged her back. "Don't let them make you choose," Gabrielle whispered. "How could you?"

Before heading home, Yellow Wing and Suzette tramped through the mud to the post store. The door was closed, but behind the window she saw a spot of candlelight. She banged on the door, and soon Monsieur Roussain was pulling them inside.

"Suzette!" he exclaimed, holding the candle high. Suzette realized how she must look: drenched, muddy, scraped. "What happened?"

She saw his open ledgers on the counter, an inkwell and pen beside them. Everything neat and tidy. She recalled his comment that morning—it seemed a lifetime ago—about running wild and remembering her French blood. But Monsieur Roussain didn't know everything. She wanted to tell him that a French girl wouldn't have been able to get out of that cave!

"I found out something about the stolen furs," she said instead, and told him what she'd discovered. Roussain listened, then fetched Captain d'Amboise and made her repeat the story.

D'Amboise listened intently, pounding his fist into his palm. "That Dupré, I knew he was up to no good."

"Will you arrest him?" Suzette asked anxiously.

"It's too dark to send my men out now. I'll have Baptiste and several of the soldiers go to the cave at first light tomorrow and seize the furs. Those beaver pelts, at least, I can claim as stolen property."

Suzette didn't care about the beaver pelts. "And you must make him tell you who traded the furs to him! I know he'll tell you it was not Papa!"

D'Amboise sighed, crouching down so he could look

directly into her face. "Suzette, I'll have Baptiste question him. But men like Dupré, they have no respect for me. I don't believe he will tell us anything."

"But can't you bring him here? Lock him up?"

"No. I can't prove that he knew the pelts were stolen. And I don't have enough soldiers to arrest every unlicensed trader I run across. All I can do is protect Fort La Pointe and try to run that scoundrel off the island for good."

"But that won't help Papa!"

Captain d'Amboise didn't answer. Yellow Wing touched her shoulder. "Come, Suzette. Let's go home."

That evening, as the story spread, people stopped by their lodge to congratulate Suzette on finding the stolen furs. It took all her energy to respond politely. Every muscle in her body ached. The ache in her heart was even worse. Finding the stolen furs didn't clear Papa's name, or keep her family from coming apart like the fluffy seeds in a milkweed pod, flying in different directions, never to meet again.

Suzette was up before dawn the next morning. Stiff and sore, she made her way to the beach in time to watch the fort men leave to confront Dupré. Baptiste led the expedition, accompanied by several soldiers, and *voyageurs* to paddle the canoes. "Don't worry, Suzette," he told her. "I'll do the best I can."

After the last faint whisper of paddle blade to water had faded away, Suzette sat by the shore. From behind her came the sounds of the waking camp: a child's wail, a dog's yelp, a *voyageur*'s laugh. She smelled wood smoke as cold fire pits were brought to life. The rain had passed. The great lake smiled this morning, lapping gently at the shore.

But Suzette couldn't find the same calm inside. *There's something I'm not seeing,* she thought. *Something I'm forgetting.* In her mind she looked again at every detail she'd seen at Dupré's camp and in the cave. Nothing. Then she listened again to the conversations she had heard between Dupré and Mikail. "Don't look for any more of those unusual beaver pelts," Dupré had scoffed. "Our man said they came from somewhere west of here—"

"Oh!" Suzette jumped to her feet, startling a gull. How could the thief—the "our man" Dupré had referred to—know where the beaver had been trapped? Monsieur Roussain hadn't written that on his inventory list. The original trapper must have told Monsieur Roussain where he had trapped the beavers when he brought the pelts to the trading post—and the thief must have overheard that conversation. It was the only way he could have known!

Suzette raced up the slope to the trading post. Roussain was just unlocking the store. "I'm surprised to see you so early, Suzette."

"*Bonjour, monsieur.*" She forced herself to speak calmly. "May I look at the ledgers?"

Roussain propped the door open with a rock: ready for business. "Of course. Study will help take your mind off things. You spend too much time out in the woods and in that canoe . . . "

Suzette had stopped listening. She found the right ledger and carefully read down each page. Halfway through, she found the entry she was looking for. A trapper named Young Star had brought the unusual beaver pelts to the post. He came on 13 March. The thirteenth sun of the moon of broken snowshoes. Ojibwe people called it that because the crusted snow often broke the netting on their snowshoes as winter struggled with spring.

Starting back at the first page, Suzette eagerly searched the ledger to see who else had hauled pelts over the frozen lake to the post on 13 March. *I know that's what happened,* she thought, tingling with excitement. *The thief overheard Young Star talking to Roussain about the pelts. That means the thief is a trapper who visited the post the same day Young Star did.*

She turned each page, carefully running a finger down the dates each trapper had visited the post. When she had gone through the whole ledger once, she turned back to the beginning and looked at every page again, checking Niskigwun's and Big Nicolas's pages with special care. But the records were clear. No other trapper had visited the post that day.

"Suzette? Shall we have a lesson today?" Monsieur

Roussain was leaning against the counter, arms folded, watching her with narrowed eyes.

She couldn't bear to sit properly on his stool, writing accounts and doing sums. "*Non, monsieur,*" she managed. "I'm sorry. I have to go back to my lodge now."

As she left the store, she looked toward the building where Papa was being held. It had no windows. Papa, as much a part of the world as the turtles and eagles and lake he so loved, locked away with no sunshine! The ache in her heart threatened to rise up her throat, steal her breath. She plodded back to the campsite.

Grandmother was alone in her lodge. Suzette paused in the doorway, nagged by a whisper of words unsaid, and waited in respectful silence.

"You may come in." Grandmother was sitting near the entrance, decorating a birch-bark box with porcupine quills.

Suzette ducked inside and knelt beside her. "I didn't have a chance to say this last night, Grandmother. I thank you for my name. A'jawac. It helped me cross the open water during the storm last night."

Grandmother nodded. "*Eya.* I saw it in my dream."

"If only I had found what I was looking for," Suzette sighed. "If only I knew who the real thief is. I don't even know if he's French or Ojibwe."

"It must have been a French man," Grandmother said, intent on her design. "Most of the French men, they are no good."

That hurt Suzette's heart. "Grandmother . . . why do you dislike the French so? Isn't my papa a good man? Wasn't your first husband?"

Grandmother paused. "*Eya*," she said finally. "Your papa is a good man. And my husband was too."

"Then why do you speak against the French? Why don't you want me to read and write their language?"

Grandmother put the box down. She was silent for so long that Suzette's annoyance faded. Whatever their differences, she respected her grandmother. She bowed her head.

Finally, Grandmother began to speak. "You know how hard it is to wait all winter for the *voyageurs* to return, not knowing if they are safe. I lost my first husband to the lake. I've seen the worry in your mother's eyes, and in yours. I would not choose that life for you."

Suzette nodded.

Grandmother was silent again for a long while before speaking. "When I was a young girl, I learned to make birch-bark baskets that were strong enough for boiling water over a fire, and so beautiful that other people asked me to make baskets for them. I learned to clean bear hides so we would have warm robes during the deep snows, and to make shirts of the softest doeskin."

Suzette smiled, imagining the young woman at work.

"After my *voyageur* husband died, I married the man you called Grandfather. Soon after we married, he became a trapper for the trading company. He was successful. He became an important man. He used his credit at the trading post to bring home warm wool blankets, and calico for shirts." Grandmother sighed. "He did not need me to make his robes. He brought home copper kettles, and no one asked for my birch-bark baskets anymore."

Suzette drew a deep breath and stared down at the intricately woven mat she was kneeling on. She tried to imagine what it must have been like for Grandmother to feel that her skills and talents were no longer important. Had it made her feel that *she* was no longer important?

"Perhaps you're too young to understand." Grandmother's voice was sad. "But times are changing. I worry that our people are becoming too dependent on the French traders."

Suzette hesitated. How could she make amends? "Grandmother . . . will you help me add some quillwork to the vest I'm making for Papa?"

Grandmother nodded slowly. "I will help you with the vest this afternoon." That was all, but Suzette could tell she was pleased.

At least I did something right today, Suzette thought, after Grandmother had gone to help a friend set up her weaving frame. Grandmother's story made her sad. At the same time, something about the story increased the feeling she'd had all morning about the stolen furs. She felt sure she was still missing something.

Hoping for more of her grandmother's wisdom, she reached into her beaver-skin pouch to touch the wild pea root Grandmother had given her the day before. As she fingered it, she realized why her grandmother's words sounded familiar. *"Times are changing,"* she breathed, her mind tumbling back to the last time she had heard those words. A new idea took shape—

No, it could not be . . . Could it?

As her mind raced, she toyed with the root. Her fingers brushed against several beads in the bottom of her pouch. For a moment she was confused. Then she remembered the spilled trade beads she'd picked up in Dupré's cave. *I must have dropped them into the pouch when I was frightened,* she thought. She pulled out the tiny glass beads and rolled them in her fingers absently, still trying to sort out another piece of the puzzle. Then she froze.

The beads were *purple.*

Suddenly they seemed to burn her skin. She stared as if she'd never seen trade beads before. The beads were exactly the color she had wanted to use in Papa's vest and could not find! Again, the faint memory of moccasins decorated with purple beads danced through her head.

Carefully, she dropped the beads back into her pouch. If only she could remember—or find—whoever had purple beadwork! That person must have traded with Dupré.

For a moment, Suzette considered trying again to search Niskigwun's and Big Nicolas's lodges. But she was becoming convinced that she had been looking in the wrong places all along. She shouldn't search for purple beadwork among the trappers' lodges.

She should search inside the fort.

Suzette slipped quickly through the trees, stopping just outside the stockade. She took a deep breath, scooping up her courage. For a moment she listened to the comforting sounds of children playing the butterfly game, hide-and-seek, nearby. *Me-e-mengwaa! Me-e-mengwaa!*

I feel as if I have memengwaa *in my belly,* Suzette thought. How could she search the men's quarters? What if she was caught? D'Amboise already believed her father was a thief. Would he suspect her of the same thing? Would she be locked away too?

One of the children darted up and grabbed her hand. "Will you play with us, Suzette?"

"No, I—" Suddenly she smiled. "Yes. I'll hide."

Surprised and delighted, the girl raced off. Suzette walked into the fort. She paused while two laborers clattered by with a handcart, then she slipped into one of the low buildings where she thought the fort men slept.

Inside the door she stopped. The small room smelled of sweat and spoiled pork. Bunks lined the walls. Weak light struggled through two windows made of thin-scraped, glazed hide. The room was a mess of clothes, blankets, snowshoes, mugs, playing cards, and dice.

Suzette hadn't taken more than a step when Captain d'Amboise suddenly appeared beside her. "What are you doing in here?" he demanded.

"Playing hide-and-seek with the children," she said quickly. "The men don't mind." Through the open door came the thin cries: "*Me-e-mengwaa! Me-e-mengwaa!*" *Butterfly, help me find my friends!*

Captain d'Amboise made a sound something like the snort of a hungry moose and threw his hands into the air. "*Mon Dieu,* how am I expected to maintain order in such a place?" he muttered. But he left her alone.

Suzette began to search the room. Finally she found the bunk and belongings of the man she was looking for. She dropped to her knees by the bed, keeping one ear cocked toward the door. Every muscle of her body was pulled tight as the basswood cords on Grandmother's weaving frame.

This man, like most of the others, kept his belongings beneath his bunk. She pawed through them hurriedly until she found a pair of ceremonial moccasins. A purple-beaded flower adorned each toe! She also found—

"What are you doing?" a voice growled behind her.

Chapter 13
Face to Face

An iron grip clamped on Suzette's arm and jerked her to her feet. "What are you doing?" Baptiste demanded again.

"I—I was playing the butterfly game," Suzette stammered. The children's cries still bounced faintly from the yard.

"You were going through my things," he growled.

The world beyond the walls seemed as far away as the moon. Anger and betrayal and fear whirled through her like leaves in an eddy. "You're hurting me," she cried, trying to pull her arm from his grasp, trying to think.

Baptiste's dark eyes glittered. His fingers bit deeper into her arm. "You—"

"Let go of her."

Baptiste whirled around, almost pulling Suzette off her feet. Monsieur Roussain was standing in the doorway.

"You can't stop me," Baptiste said after a moment.

Roussain looked sad. "My friend, let go of her. You don't want to hurt Suzette, and you don't want to hurt me."

If Baptiste hadn't been holding her, Suzette would have thrown her arms around the clerk. "How did you know I was here?"

"I watched you looking at the ledger this morning," Roussain explained, his gaze never leaving Baptiste's face. "Your finger was running down the date column. And I remembered you saying that the thief had told Dupré the furs came from the west. After you left, I thought more about it and realized what you had been looking for. So I checked the ledger too. No one else came into the post the day Young Star brought in those unusual furs. But I wasn't alone that day." He pointed at Baptiste. "You were there. You heard Young Star tell me where the furs came from. No one else could have known that."

Time seemed to stop. Suzette was astonished to hear the children still at play, the distant shout of a laborer. Her arm was getting numb—

Baptiste threw Suzette aside and leaped for the door. Roussain dove to stop him. The thin clerk was knocked to the ground, but he managed to pull Baptiste down too.

Suzette knew Roussain was no match for Baptiste. As Baptiste struggled to his feet, she lunged. She slammed to the floor, but she was able to wrap her arms around his legs. "Help!" she screamed, trying desperately to hang on.

Suddenly Baptiste stopped kicking. Suzette looked up

and saw Captain d'Amboise, flanked by three of his soldiers. Two of them were holding Baptiste. She and Monsieur Roussain untangled themselves and scrambled to their feet.

Captain d'Amboise didn't even wait for an explanation. "That was a clever plan, telling my men to stay behind on Dupré's little island this morning while you came back here," he said to Baptiste. Every word was clipped and tight. "Fortunately, they knew they didn't have to take such orders from you. After you disappeared, they had the *voyageurs* paddle them back here. What is going on?"

Suzette couldn't wait any longer. "I think Baptiste stole the furs!"

"Your father has already confessed," Baptiste said disdainfully, then looked at Captain d'Amboise. "Philippe Choudoir is the thief!"

"I don't think so," Roussain said, and told the captain what Suzette had discovered about the stolen furs.

"And I overheard Mikail and Dupré talking," Suzette added eagerly. "Mikail was unhappy that you sent a soldier along to visit the camp, instead of sending Baptiste alone. And look at these!" She handed Baptiste's moccasins to Captain d'Amboise. "Only Dupré carries purple beads. I knew whoever had these moccasins must have traded with Dupré. Monsieur Roussain does not have such beads."

Captain d'Amboise shook his head. "*Mon Dieu,* Baptiste. You've been dealing with Dupré for some time?"

"There's more." Suzette knelt and reached under Baptiste's bed. Carefully she pulled out three clean new traps. "These have never been used," she pointed out. "If you look at Monsieur Roussain's ledger, I don't think you'll find any entries for traps sold to Baptiste. I think Baptiste traded the stolen furs to Dupré for the traps and goods he needs to head west on his own. That's what he wants—"

"So I wanted to leave!" Baptiste exclaimed, facing d'Amboise. "Is that so hard to believe? I *had* to steal those furs! You never let me have enough time to trap on my own. I watch everyone around me profit, yet I'm expected to be content with the small amount of trade goods the company provides in exchange for my work." His face twisted. "You've never been fair to me. It's because I am mixed-blood. *Métis.*"

The words hung in the air like breath on a deep-winter day. *He did this because he was Métis?* Suzette thought, suddenly cold inside.

But d'Amboise shook his head sadly. "*Non,* Baptiste. It means nothing to me if you are French, *Métis,* or Ojibwe. The problems are all in your head. You are looking for someone to blame. Well, blame yourself. I am a fair man. I'm a fair man, and you betrayed my trust."

Baptiste spat on the ground. "I have betrayed nothing."

A flame of rage flared in Suzette. "You've betrayed *me!*" she blazed. "How could you do such a terrible thing? How could you make it look like Papa had been the thief?" A new thought struck. Had Baptiste been on the mainland the night before her family crossed to the island? "And the canoe?" she demanded. "Did *you* damage Papa's canoe?"

The confusion in Baptiste's eyes was too real to disbelieve. "I don't know anything about Philippe's canoe. As for the rest . . ."

Suzette's anger died as quickly as it had flamed to life, leaving her voice hurt and thin. "But *why?* Why did you do this to Papa, Baptiste? Why did you do this to my family?"

"I never meant to." Baptiste stared at the ground, finally sounding ashamed. "They had already started to suspect Philippe before I found his crucifix. It was so easy to leave that little cross and one of the striped furs where I knew they would be found—"

"Take him away." Captain d'Amboise jerked his head at the soldiers.

Suzette grabbed the captain's sleeve. "And you will let Papa go now?"

He laughed, the storm clouds driven from his face. "*Oui,* Suzette. I will."

Soon Papa was sitting in front of his lodge. "I am so proud of you, Suzette," he said again, as Mama handed him a bowl of his favorite, specially seasoned pea soup. As word of his release trickled through the camp, many friends stopped by to wish him well.

Papa was relaxing with his pipe that afternoon, surrounded by his family, when Captain d'Amboise and Monsieur Roussain walked up. "I hope we're not intruding," d'Amboise said. He held himself stiffly, as though he felt ill at ease.

Suzette thought she saw resentment flicker in Papa's blue eyes. Then he gestured with his arm. "Welcome to my lodge." She breathed a sigh of relief as d'Amboise and Roussain sat down by the fire. Mama and Grandmother quietly prepared bowls of food to offer their guests.

"I can only say I'm sorry, Philippe, for everything that happened." Captain d'Amboise leaned over and put out his hand in the French manner. "I made the best decisions I knew how to make. I had to take action."

Papa accepted his hand and shook it solemnly. "I would have thought that you knew me too well to believe I could do such a thing."

"You didn't help by telling us you were the one we were looking for." D'Amboise clearly wanted an explanation.

Papa shrugged. "You threatened Yellow Wing too. It seemed clear you were intent on taking me. I had to make sure my family was taken care of. I trusted Yellow Wing to do that." He translated for his brother-in-law, who nodded.

"What will happen to Baptiste?" Yellow Wing asked then, and Papa repeated the question in French.

"What I promised. I will hold him for fourteen days, then send him away from the island. There is nothing more

I can do. He will be welcome in this region no more."

Roussain added sadly, "Baptiste is not at heart a bad man. He is a confused and unhappy man."

"He blamed his troubles on being *Métis,*" Suzette said quietly. Remembering Baptiste's words made her feel uneasy. Was being *Métis* such a heavy load to carry?

Captain d'Amboise filled the silence. "Suzette, I want to thank you for everything you did. I know you did it to clear your papa. But I hate to think of any injustice being done at Fort La Pointe while I am in command. You kept that from happening."

"You found answers when the rest of us failed," Monsieur Roussain added. "When I think of what you did, how you figured things through . . . I am amazed."

"I have been well taught," she said modestly. "My family has taught me to be safe in the woods, and to paddle a canoe, and to be observant. And you, *monsieur,* taught me how to read French." She said the words in Ojibwe and then in French, thinking it all over.

Suddenly she caught her breath. "Do you know what I just realized?" she said slowly. "I could not have found the answer if I was only French or only Ojibwe. I needed to know how to read the ledgers. And I needed to know how to take care of myself in the woods and in a canoe. I was only able to clear Papa's name because I am *Métis.*" A warmth spread through her, like the warmth of a new sunrise over *Lac Supérieur,* pushing away the shadows.

"Baptiste was wrong. Being *Métis* can be wonderful."

Monsieur Roussain smiled. "All right, Suzette. I'll stop trying to turn you into a French girl. But I still expect you for lessons."

Grandmother wasn't willing to say quite as much. But she nodded too. "And don't forget, Granddaughter. Later, we will practice your quillwork."

"*Oui. Eya*," Suzette said to them both, unable to hide her own grin.

Captain d'Amboise nodded thoughtfully. "Suzette, I do not doubt that living in two worlds as you do is difficult. It will probably always be difficult, in some ways. But the time when Indian people lived here and white people lived somewhere else is past. More white people are going to come to this land. To trade. Perhaps even to farm the land."

Suzette wasn't sure what "farm the land" meant, but she didn't interrupt.

"We are going to need people like you. *Métis* people. People who understand both worlds and can help other people understand. Well." He pushed to his feet. "Philippe, I will leave you to your family." Roussain followed.

Then d'Amboise looked back. "And don't forget, Philippe. You have until tomorrow at high sun to turn in any remaining furs for the competition."

Suzette clapped a hand over her mouth. The trappers' competition! She had forgotten all about it.

CHAPTER 14
THE COMPETITION

The next day, Papa took the last of his furs to the fort. "Well, that's done," he said when he returned to the family's camp. "Now we just wait and see." He sat on the ground and reached for his tobacco pouch. "There's still one thing bothering me, though. Who damaged our canoe?"

"Are you sure it wasn't an accident?" Suzette asked. She was twisting nettle stalk fibers into twine for Mama.

"I know my canoe."

Suzette couldn't argue with that. She changed the subject. "Papa . . . all this trouble's made me think about something. I know you'll have to go to Montréal for the winter if you don't win the competition. But—" She gathered her courage, looking at her mother, who was playing with Charlotte nearby. "Do you ever think about going back for good?"

Mama dropped the bright ribbon she'd been dangling

for the baby and looked up sharply. Papa's eyes widened. "Why would I do that, when my family is here?"

"Because you are French!"

"*Oui,* I am French, but *this* is my home." Papa looked intently into Suzette's eyes. "My family is here."

"But you have family in Montréal too," Suzette said stubbornly. She needed to know.

"Suzette." Mama's tone said, *Respect your papa. Don't argue with him.*

Papa sighed. "It's all right, Shining Stone. She has a right to ask. Yes, Suzette, I have family in Montréal." He leaned against a tree, puffing his pipe. "As you know, I argued with them when I was a young man. They wanted to choose the path for my life. I chose another. I am content with my choice. But I do still think about my family there from time to time."

Suzette sat still as a heron watching for fish, wanting to hear more.

"Sometimes I wish you could meet them." Papa stared away from the lodge, through the camp, perhaps seeing sights far beyond the great lake. "But I know in my heart that you would not be made welcome in Montréal. My parents and brothers—everyone would try to change you, turn you into something you're not. And they would have no wish to come to La Pointe. *Non,* our place is here."

Suzette felt a burden of worry slide away. Her parents were not going to force her to choose who she was or where she belonged. Papa had already been forced to make that painful choice. *Papa chose us,* she thought. *Papa chose us.*

Suzette spent part of the afternoon with Grandmother, preparing porcupine quills for fancywork. Grandmother showed her how to flatten them between two bones and told her which plants could be used to dye them soft shades of purple and yellow and pink. Then she helped Suzette make a small design on Papa's vest.

But Suzette couldn't stop thinking about the competition and everything it meant to her family. Later, feeling restless, she asked Mama if she could go visiting. "Of course," Mama said, smiling. "Be sure to invite your friends to the feast we're planning to celebrate Papa's release."

Suzette had two visits to make. She felt guilty for suspecting Niskigwun and Big Nicolas of the theft. She needed to make things right.

Choosing to get the least pleasant visit over with first, she wound through the meadow toward Niskigwun's lodge at the far end of the camp. *"Aaniin,"* Suzette called as she approached, but the fire pit was cold, the lodge deserted.

As she turned to go, Two Fish emerged from the forest path. He was carrying a quiver of arrows and his bow, and over his shoulder, a new-killed doe. *Blue Eyes!* Suddenly

Two Fish's insult seemed silly and hollow, and she was even more ashamed of her own taunt. "I'm sorry I called you Dakota boy, Two Fish," she said quickly.

He blinked and let the deer slide to the ground. A chickadee chittered at them from a nearby branch. "I'm sorry I was not kind to you, too," he mumbled. He stared at the toes of his worn moccasins, looking much as Baptiste had the day before. "I was trying to apologize, the day you—you called me that. I had heard your father was in trouble. It made me feel bad."

Suzette nodded, relieved. "We will forget it now, *eya?*" She took a breath. "We're having a feast tonight. I came to ask your father if he—if both of you—would join us."

Two Fish blinked again. "I'll tell him," he said finally. "It will be an honor."

So why did he still look miserable? Silly boy! Suzette turned to go.

"Wait! I—I have something to tell you." Two Fish swallowed hard. "I did a bad thing. On the mainland. The night before you crossed, I . . . I took my knife to your canoe. I scraped away some of the pitch."

"It was *you?*" Suzette gasped.

"I'm sorry! I'm sorry! I didn't think anyone would get hurt. I just thought your papa would throw some of his furs overboard. When I heard later that you went in, I felt very bad." His chin drooped toward his chest. "It's been like a wolf, chewing at my insides."

"But why?" Suzette demanded. "Why did you do it?"

"It was for my father! I thought that if he won the competition, people would respect him more. People are mean to him because of my mother."

Suzette felt her cheeks burn. *People like me,* she thought. She scuffed the ground with one toe. "I'm sorry. We'll try to mend some things tonight," she said finally.

His eyes widened. "You mean we're still welcome?"

Suzette nodded. "Yes. Come when you're ready." She left Two Fish staring after her.

Her next visit was to Big Nicolas. She found him in the *voyageurs'* camp, playing a gambling game. He jumped to his feet when he saw her. "Suzette! I stopped by your lodge a while ago, but I missed you and your papa. Please tell him how happy I was to hear the good news."

"I hope you can tell him yourself!" Suzette grinned. "We would like you to join us for a feast this evening. Whenever you are hungry, come by."

He pulled off his dirty red stocking cap and smacked it against his palm. "I'll be there! We'll celebrate in style, eh?"

"*Oui.*" Then she found herself blurting out the question she hadn't planned to ask. "Big Nicolas . . . one day I saw you and Niskigwun coming around the point in a canoe. It didn't look like you'd been fishing." She felt her cheeks get warm. "I just wondered—what were you doing together?"

If he thought her question rude, he was too kind to show it. "You know since I broke my arm, I can no longer work as a *voyageur.*" His voice held a hint of sadness, but he pushed on quickly. "I spent the winter trapping, hoping to earn passage back to Montréal. But in truth, I do not want to go back to Montréal. I like it here."

Suzette smiled again. She understood that feeling.

"So I think to myself, what do I do now? I could stay here and trap, but—bah. That is a sad life for a canoe man. So I think some more. Perhaps I'll start a farm, here on La Pointe. I grew up on a farm. I know of such things."

Suzette reminded herself to ask Papa what a farm was.

"Or maybe I'll try to mine copper." He shrugged. "I don't know. And I don't know the land very well. So I asked Niskigwun to take me on a tour. Niskigwun is strong. He doesn't mind paddling with a man who has a weak arm."

And perhaps he liked being asked for a favor by a friendly man, Suzette thought. She nodded at Big Nicolas. "Thank you for telling me. We'll look for you at the feast."

By late afternoon, many friends were seated on the ground near Suzette's lodge. Some brought food and other gifts in honor of Philippe's release. Papa and Mama, in turn, gave gifts to their friends. Suzette gave Gabrielle a new bracelet. The girls were honored for having the strength and courage to dig out of the cave and paddle back to La Pointe, and everyone feasted on the fresh trout and venison Yellow Wing had provided. Big Nicolas's booming laugh often rang over all the noise. Niskigwun and Two Fish were there too. Suzette saw Big Nicolas draw Niskigwun into a circle of men to hear a joke, and smiled.

When the sun finally slid behind the western waters, Suzette and her family walked to the landing and watched the *voyageurs* build two big bonfires. As a blanket of stars appeared overhead, the post carpenter brought out his fiddle and played one lively jig after another. Several Ojibwe men kept time on their drums. "I feel like it's the first night of *rendez-vous,*" Suzette exclaimed, and felt Papa squeeze her shoulder. Sometimes the musicians took a rest and the *voyageurs* sang, leaning close to provide harmony, bellowing their songs so they rang across the water. Sometimes Ojibwe people offered a song instead.

And the people danced: hopping jigs, shuffling line marches, exuberant made-up dances. Because there were more men than women, some of the *voyageurs* danced with each other or with their precious paddles. One of the *Métis* women even coaxed Monsieur Roussain, who *never* danced, to join her in a reel.

Suzette danced her share, but soon she slipped to the side so she could watch. The moon and the roaring fires shed light on the dancers. She saw a colorful mixture of European and Indian clothes and heard a happy babble of Ojibwe, French, and other languages too. Leaning back on her elbows, she soaked it all in.

She heard a boisterous laugh and caught sight of Papa, standing with some of his friends. He looked very handsome in his breeches and beaded moccasins, the sash Mama had made, and the top hat he'd worn as a steersman in the big Montréal canoes. He was wearing his new vest, too. Suzette thought it was perfect: some quillwork, some beading . . . in a lovely blue design.

A moment later, when the fiddler began another lively tune, Papa grabbed his wife's hand and whirled her around, laughing all the while. Suzette felt a sudden lump in her throat, and tucked the image away in her heart. *I wish Papa and Mama could always be so happy,* she thought, and knew it was not to be. If Papa didn't win the competition, he would spend his winter in Montréal, and Mama would spend the cold months waiting. Even if Papa did win, as wonderful as that would be, it meant he would spend the rest of his winters trapping. *That is a sad life for a canoe man,* Big Nicolas had said, and Suzette knew it was true.

When the party was well under way, Captain d'Amboise walked down from the stockade, dressed in his finest French clothes. It took a few moments to get everyone quiet. Then two laborers hoisted him on top of a barrel.

"As you know, the fur trappers' competition came to a close today," d'Amboise shouted. "Despite our recent . . . problems, I have every confidence that our competition was fair. A good thing, too, for the top three trappers were very close."

The crowd pushed closer. A breeze blew in from the lake, ruffling Suzette's hair. She held her breath, waiting.

"The winner is . . . Niskigwun!"

Suzette let out her breath slowly. D'Amboise held up his hands for quiet. "At final count, Niskigwun had more credits than any other trapper. Philippe Choudoir and Nicolas Lemieux were very close behind. I will give them extra credit at the store to equal three beaver pelts."

So. It was decided. Without the prize to pay his debt, Papa would leave with the *voyageurs*. A year of hard work, for nothing. This winter, when the long white days stretched endlessly into long cold nights, Papa would be far away. He would be in a place Suzette could not even imagine, surrounded by people who would not accept his wife or children.

The carpenter struck up his fiddle again, but Suzette was in no mood for dancing now. She circled the crowd until she spotted the rest of her family. Papa had his arms around his wife. "It's all right, Shining Stone," he was saying, although his voice did not sound like it was all right, not at all. When he saw Suzette, he pulled her into the hug too. "Don't be too sad, *mignonne*," he whispered into her hair. "I will be back again in the spring, eh? I promise."

Several of the *voyageurs* came by and slapped Papa on the shoulder, as if to say, *Sorry, Philippe. We know this is not what you want. But we will be glad to have you with us again.*

Niskigwun shouldered his way through the crowd. Papa raised his chin and held out his hand. "Congratulations, Niskigwun," he said. "You are a fine trapper."

Niskigwun accepted his handshake. "And you are as well. You made the challenge worthwhile." He nodded once, then disappeared again. Suzette unclenched her fists, thankful Niskigwun had been so gracious.

Papa took a deep breath. "Well, let's enjoy the party," he said, and Suzette could tell he was trying to sound hearty. "We have had too many sad evenings. Let's—"

"Philippe!" Captain d'Amboise emerged from the shadows. "I've been looking for you. May I talk to you? And your family?"

Silently, they followed the commander away from the noise and commotion. When they could talk without shouting, d'Amboise got right to it. "Philippe, since Baptiste is no longer in my employ, I have a problem. I have no interpreter."

Suzette caught her breath.

"You speak Ojibwe well," d'Amboise continued. "You can handle a canoe. You are at home in the woods. The job is yours, if you want it."

Suzette waited for Papa to whoop with joy. Instead he stared at d'Amboise as if struck dumb. "But what about my debt?" he asked finally.

"Philippe, you're a good man," d'Amboise said, waving his hand. "I had hoped you would win the competition, and that would be the end of your debt. Since that did not happen . . . and in light of the recent trouble . . . I am going to personally cover your debt. Your loan is now with me. In exchange for your services as interpreter, you will receive enough in trade to care for your family. When you have spare time, you can trap. Anything you bring in, we'll apply toward your debt." He looked Papa in the eye. "I trust you, my friend."

Papa still looked dazed. "I see . . ."

"Your family can live on the island year-round, if they wish," d'Amboise went on. "It would probably be best if they did. You'll have to be away from your family for sometimes two or three weeks at a time, paddling down the inland rivers to reach some of the farthest camps—"

"You mean I can still paddle the rivers?"

D'Amboise nodded, starting to grin.

"And I'll spend most of the year with my family?"

"Yes!" Captain d'Amboise laughed.

"Whoooaaah!" Papa howled. He began to dance. He whirled Mama until she was laughing and breathless. He grabbed Grandmother's hands and led her in a stately march up and down. He pulled Charlotte to his shoulder, gently dipping and bobbing. After passing the baby back to Grandmother, he snatched Suzette from the ground, spinning until the world raced dizzily around them and she was shrieking with laughter. When he finally set her down, he reached for his wife again.

Suzette clapped in time with the beat, watching her parents dance. She was happy. She was home.

A Peek into the Past

Looking Back: 1732

Ojibwe families made their own birch-bark canoes for traveling.

Ojibwe people have lived in what is now northern Wisconsin for hundreds of years. French travelers were the first Europeans to visit the region, arriving less than 100 years before Suzette's story takes place.

Ojibwe families lived by the seasons. In fall, they canoed through wetlands to harvest wild rice. During the long winters, they lived in small camps deep in the woods so they could hunt and trap, and in spring they tapped maple trees for sap to make into sugar. In summer, they settled in large villages, planting gardens and fishing in nearby waters.

At the time of Suzette's story, as many as 2,000 Ojibwe people summered on La Pointe Island. They called it *Moningwanekaaning*, Place of Many Golden-Breasted Woodpeckers. It had been their summer gathering place for generations. Ojibwes still consider it an important place today.

*Ojibwe people built **wiigwams**, or lodges, at a summer campsite.*

French people built the first trading post on the island in the 1690s. They established a brisk trade with the Ojibwe, offering manufactured goods such as cloth, weapons, and metal tools in exchange for the furs of beaver, fox, bear, and other animals. Furs were in great demand in Europe, to be made into fashionable clothing and tall hats for gentlemen.

The French began the fur trade long before they reached La Pointe. It started in the late 1500s, when the French began trading with tribes in eastern Canada, such as the Huron, Cree, and Micmac.

By the 1600s, the fur trade was so valuable that the French government established laws to control it. Only traders with government licenses could form companies and trade with Indians. As the French pushed west along the St. Lawrence River and the Great Lakes, the fur trade grew to include more tribes, including the Ojibwe.

All along the vast fur-trade route, skilled men from many tribes spent their winters tracking animals. Once the animals had been killed and skinned, Indian women and girls cleaned and dried the pelts. Indian men then took the furs to the nearest fort and traded them for European

Indians traded furs for French goods such as kettles, earbobs, and beads.

A beaver pelt stretched on a wood frame to dry

Ledger pages

goods. A clerk from the trading company recorded each transaction in a *ledger*, or notebook, just as Monsieur Roussain does.

The fur-trade companies hired strong, adventurous men called *voyageurs* to paddle huge canoes to the forts to collect the furs. The *voyageurs* traveled more than 2,500 miles round-trip each year. They left the French-Canadian city of Montréal in early spring, paddled to forts on the western frontier, and returned to Montréal before the rivers froze over. In Montréal, the furs were loaded onto sailing ships bound for Europe.

The *voyageurs'* route took them along treacherous rivers, through vast forests, and across the Great Lakes. The largest canoes held 16 paddlers and 8,000 pounds—four tons—of cargo! *Voyageurs* worked 14 hours a day, paddling hard the whole time. They

kept the pace by singing as they paddled, and their songs rang over the water. When rivers were impassable, *voyageurs* carried their canoes and cargo many miles over rough trails.

Voyageurs paddling through rapids

Like Suzette's papa, most *voyageurs* loved contests, songs, and colorful clothes. At forts like La Pointe, their arrival was a highlight of the year, wildly celebrated with feasting, singing, and dancing.

The fur trade lasted more than 250 years and eventually included Indian tribes all the way to the Pacific Ocean. The French controlled the trade until 1760, and then it passed to the British, and finally to the Americans.

he voyageurs' annual arrival sparked wild celebrations.

The fur trade brought together very different cultures and had a huge impact on Native American people. French traders and *voyageurs* often married Indian women. In fact, La Pointe Island is known today as Madeline Island in honor of a chief's daughter who married a prominent trader. Many *voyageur* husbands not only loved their families but also embraced Indian life, as Suzette's father does. Other marriages were mainly

This Métis woman wears European-style clothes with Indian blanket and jewelry.

A Métis girl's doll, its face painted brown

business arrangements. In either case, mixed marriages created partnerships that helped each person understand the other culture.

Children of Indian-French marriages, like Suzette and Gabrielle, were called *Métis*. Because *Métis* people understood both Indian and white culture, they often served as go-betweens. Many became leaders in fur-trading communities. A few *Métis* women even became respected traders after their husbands died.

As long as the fur trade lasted, French and Indian people depended on and learned from each other. Yet the cultures sometimes clashed. Traditional women's skills, like decorating clothing with porcupine quills and making baskets and sturdy birch-bark containers, lost favor when European goods such as kettles and beads became popular. Such changes saddened women like Suzette's grandmother, whose traditional skills were no longer so valued.

Quilled moccasin (above) and beaded moccasin (below)

The fur trade also damaged the traditional ways that tribal members took care of each other and the environment. Instead of sharing extra food or goods with other members of the tribe, trappers learned to work for personal gain and to spend their earnings on themselves, as Europeans did. And the fur trade encouraged Indian men to trap too many animals. Over time, the populations of beaver and other animals fell dramatically, and families that depended on the fur trade struggled to survive.

Life for Ojibwe and *Métis* people changed even more in the 1800s. As white women and families began to settle in the region, mixed marriages became less acceptable to the traders. Ugly prejudice arose against Native Americans and *Métis*. Trying to find acceptance, many *Métis* decided to live as only white or only Indian, denying the other part of their background.

Harsh prejudice lasted for more than a century, but Ojibwe culture survived. Today, many Ojibwe people, and people of mixed heritage, live in the Lake Superior region. Although they live modern lifestyles, the traditions and values of their ancestors are still honored.

Modern-day Ojibwe girls get ready to dance at a powwow.

GLOSSARY OF FRENCH WORDS

bonjour *(bohn-zhoor)*—hello

chocolat *(sho-ko-lah)*—chocolate

Comment allez-vous? *(ko-mahn tah-lay voo)*—How are you?

imbécile *(ehm-bay-seel)*—idiot

la crosse *(lah krohs)*—a game similar to field hockey, played with a ball and long sticks that have a net on one end

Lac Supérieur *(lahk soo-pay-ree-yur)*—Lake Superior

loutre *(loo-truh)*—otter

merci *(mehr-see)*—thank you

mes amis *(may-zah-mee)*—my friends

Métis *(may-tee)*—a person of mixed French and Indian heritage

mignonne *(mee-nyun)*—darling (used for a girl or woman)

Mon Dieu! *(mohn dyuh)*—Good heavens!

monsieur *(muh-syer)*—Mister or sir

non *(nohn)*—no

oui *(wee)*—yes

pardonnez-moi *(pahr-dohn-nay mwa)*—excuse me

rendez-vous *(rahn-day-voo)*—a meeting. During the fur trade, this word became the name for the annual gathering of *voyageurs,* fur trappers, and traders.

très bien *(tray byen)*—very good

voyageur *(vwoy-yah-zhur)*—a traveler, especially a man hired to transport goods along the fur-trade route

GLOSSARY OF OJIBWE WORDS

aaniin *(aah-neen)*—hello. (Today most Ojibwe people use a different greeting, *boozhoo,* which evolved from the French word *bonjour.*)

bagaadowe *(bah-GAH-doh-way)*—a game now known by the French name *la crosse,* played with a ball and netted stick

eya *(eh-YAH)*—yes. (This word is used only by girls and women.)

Gizhe Manido *(gih-ZHAY mahn-ih-DOH)*—Great Spirit

maawanji'iwin *(maah-wahn-JIH-ih-win)*—a gathering

makak *(mah-KAHK)*—a small birch-bark container

memengwaa *(meh-meng-GWAA)*—butterfly

miigwech *(mee-GWETCH)*—thank you

Moningwanekaaning *(mo-NING-wah-NAY-kawn-ing)*— The Ojibwe name for La Pointe Island (now called Madeline Island). It means "Place of Many Golden-Breasted Woodpeckers." The Ojibwe chose this name because so many golden-breasted woodpeckers, or flickers, lived there.

Ojibwe *(o-JIB-way)*—the name of a large group of Native American people who live in the Lake Superior region

watab *(wah-TAHB)*—fibers split from the roots of small evergreen trees, used to sew sheets of birch bark together over canoe frames

wiigwam *(WEEG-wahm)*—an Ojibwe lodge with birch-bark covering

Author's Note

For this story, I simplified the description of the *voyageurs'* annual trip to Fort La Pointe. Most likely, the voyageurs paddled from Montréal to a large trading center at Fort Michilimackinac, in Lake Michigan, before going on to La Pointe later in the summer.

Like the other characters, Captain d'Amboise and Monsieur Roussain are fictional. The real commander at Fort La Pointe in 1732 was Jacques Legardeur de Saint-Pierre. The Gull Rock mentioned in the story is also fictional. A small island once existed off the eastern shore of La Pointe, but it has since eroded and disappeared.

Today a visit to the Madeline Island Historical Museum in La Pointe, Wisconsin, and the nearby Big Bay State and Town Parks will provide a good sense of the island's history. To learn more about the region's Ojibwe history, I recommend visiting Waswagoning, an Ojibwe Indian village, and the George W. Brown Jr. Ojibwe Museum and Cultural Center, both in Lac du Flambeau, Wisconsin.